THE IDENTITY ENIGMA

LIS MCDERMOTT

This edition published in 2024 by Westwater Publishing

ISBN 978-1-7394507-6-2 (paperback 1st edition)
ISBN 978-1-7394507-5-5 (ebook 1st edition)

Dedicated to Conrad

PROLOGUE: FEBRUARY 2019
HAVERIGG, CUMBRIA

I breathed in deeply, inhaling the air of freedom. The prison car park was surprisingly busy for this time of day. In the smaller public section, a local woman lost the battle to calm her excitable dog while at the same time attempting to attach its lead, before setting off for a walk in the fields opposite. It had been some months since I'd had a visit out, so I'd forgotten some of the locals made use of the large car park. Today it was dull and cold and the westerly wind whipped around the corner of buildings, across the fields from the sea, and down the road leading to the village – far more hospitable conditions than I'd endured for the last three years.

A sound caught my attention, coming from the direction where the woman with the dog had parked. I noticed a sleek black car, whose driver had just turned on the ignition, leaving the engine idling. Turning towards the car with some trepidation, I felt my anxiety subside as soon as I saw Jaz open the driver's door and wave.

I walked over to him, and after we greeted each other like long-lost brothers, he took my bag from me and threw it into the car boot as I climbed into the passenger seat.

"You okay?" Jaz asked.

"Relieved to be out of that hell-hole, yeah."

"It doesn't look much like a hell-hole, not compared with where Dad's seeing out his time."

"The scenery may be prettier, but believe me, the guys inside are just as evil and hard as steel." I glanced around, already feeling the knot in my stomach untangling. "Is everything planned?"

Jaz nodded. "You still want to go through with this, or have you had a change of heart?"

"No. It's the only thing I can do to make sure my family are safe. And I want to stay alive too. Did you manage to get the papers for me?"

"Yeah, I'll show you when we get clear of here. I'm hoping no one will notice us together."

Jaz set off, driving us away from the prison as fast as he could without breaking the speed limits. From there, he drove the short distance to the local car rental unit. Initially, I'd thought it a weird place to have a car rental, but having seen how remote the prison was, I recognised they probably had a pretty good stream of customers. Jaz parked away from the entrance again, not wanting to draw attention to the pair of us.

Once parked, he stretched over to the back seat so he could retrieve the papers he had promised. Handing them over, he asked, "What do you think, Mr Sam Duncan?"

I perused the documents carefully: passport, driving licence, bank accounts, bank cards – everything I would need. Checking for faults but finding none, as the new 'Sam Duncan'. Impressed, I said, "They're perfect. I can't see anything wrong with them, but that doesn't mean that customs won't."

Jaz also handed me a large package. "The £46 discharge grant won't get you very far!"

There must have been at least a couple of thousand pounds, if not more.

"Shit, Jaz. I didn't expect this."

"You never got paid for the work you did for my dad. So, this would have been your share. There's money in your bank account, so as long as you don't burn it in one go, you should be able to manage for some time. And before you say anything, part of me is grateful you turned my dad in, because it means I can get my life back on track, too."

"Thanks, man. I owe you so much." I hugged Jaz close.

He pulled away, smiling. "You've no need to worry about your documents. They're fine. Anyway, they won't be looking for you. You're not wanted, and nobody is going to look at you twice, as long as you keep your cool."

"Yeah, I suppose so."

"You know I've wanted to get out of this life for so long, and now that Dad's inside, with most of his crew, I can go anywhere in the world and start again. I've nothing to lose, and now, nobody who is relying on me to stay. How do you feel about leaving people behind, your family and your girl?" he said, looking up at me.

"I'm trying not to think about it, so thanks for reminding me." I thumped him on his shoulder. "I know I'm doing the right thing. So, let's get on with it."

As I walked away from the car, Jaz called out. "Hey, Sam."

Initially, I didn't answer, until I remembered he was calling me! Jaz gave me a sideways glance.

"Make sure you sign for the car in your real identity, not the new one," he said. "Hey, and don't smile like a nutter while you're driving. You're supposed to be depressed."

"Thanks. I know I'm stupid, but not that stupid. Anyway, I need to practise signing the new name before I use it." Giving him a purposefully inane smile, I disappeared into the car rental office.

A little while later, I drove my small rented hatchback out of the entrance. Jaz turned on his ignition and followed, before taking over to get in the lead. I'd shared a destination with him that one of my old cell mates had told me about. Jaz had planned a route where there were few traffic cameras, and where we could travel unnoticed.

After about an hour and a half, as the sun began to disappear behind the horizon, we arrived at our destination: the secluded *B*-road that ran alongside the Irish Sea at Allonby Bay. The landscape was flat and grey, with an inhospitable coldness that tore in from the sea and nudged my little car as I drove. As a sign to me, Jaz signalled left but continued driving. I pulled over and drove off the road onto the muddy layby, before bumping down across a slightly larger dip than expected onto the gravelly beach below. There wasn't a soul around, and the nearest house, situated several hundred feet away, stood in complete darkness. There were no streetlights along the entire stretch, so the only illumination came from my headlights and a distant glimmer from some dim buildings beyond.

The little car jolted over the pebbles and rocks before coming to a standstill about a hundred yards from where the tide reached before it returned to the depths. I removed all my clothes, and my shoes, then piled them on the passenger seat along with any identification I had in my old name, along with my 'goodbye' note. Lastly, I remembered to leave car keys in the ignition.

Even though the cold began to seep into my bones, I sat for some time, looking out at the mesmerising movement of the darkening waves as they ebbed and flowed, trickling across the shingle. I couldn't ever imagine feeling so low that I'd actually consider killing myself, but then I wondered if I was being over optimistic about my future. Could I really escape my past? A shiver ran through my body. Hearing a car coming towards my position, I hurriedly climbed out of mine and crouched beside it.

As the car briefly shone some light in my direction, I recognised it as Jaz returning down the road. He drove past, did a U-turn, and came back. The cold began to penetrate my skin as I sprinted across the beach's sharp surface, leapt into the back seat, and pulled on the new, warm clothes Jaz had ready for me.

Taking the next right turn, now in the complete darkness of night, Jaz drove us to Penrith, where we rested before driving on the next morning.

Someone – hopefully the police – would find my empty car, the clothes I'd been wearing as I'd walked out of prison, plus the suicide note, and hopefully assume I'd walked into the sea. Eventually, I would be presumed dead, my old life extinguished.

1

APRIL 2023
STOCKHOLM

Emerging from customs, tired and hungry, having not eaten much during the day, Kyra scanned the many faces of those waiting in arrivals at Arlanda Airport, and instantly panicked. Nils wasn't there. She couldn't see him anywhere, and with his height, he wasn't someone you could miss. Had she got it so wrong? Another passenger bumped into her as she stopped suddenly in her tracks. Apologising, Kyra began walking towards the large space full of welcoming faces, but not the one she wanted to see.

Heaving her backpack onto her shoulders, she wandered to a quieter spot to decide what to do. Desperately, she hunted through her bag for her mobile. Before she found it, she heard her name. She looked up and saw Nils frantically waving at her. Relieved, she rushed towards him, swerving between huggers, people chatting and piles of abandoned luggage lying in wait to trip her up, before throwing herself into his arms. He pulled her tight into his body in an all-embracing bear hug and bent down to kiss her.

"My gift is here at last. Can we get home so I can unwrap it?"

He gave her a cheeky grin, then stepped away from her, pre-empting the slap he probably half expected to come his way.

"I thought you'd forgotten me."

"I'm sorry, the metro was on a go-slow."

"Can we eat first? I'm so hungry?" Kyra asked.

"But it's been four years that I've been waiting." Nils gave her a mock pleading look.

"Surely you can wait just a little longer. I mean, the pandemic wasn't down to me, I didn't start it." Kyra smiled and stretched up to kiss him again, enjoying the warmth of his lips. "You might just get an extra-special dessert, if you're good."

Nils grabbed her backpack, and taking her hand so they could move through the crowded airport as one, led the way to the Arlanda Express on which they'd travel into Stockholm city, where they'd catch a metro to near Nils' apartment.

It had been four years ago that Kyra had promised Nils she would thank him for his help with the research into the Swedish family descendant involved in the Aliciana mystery. After his father's death at sea, James Anderson, the CEO of Andersson Global, had given her an exclusive interview, and the consequent article she had written had been picked up by several national newspapers. Then a whole load of work had come her way, followed closely by the pandemic that put the whole world on hold. On top of that, family issues had taken up her time too. Now, having just finished her latest research project and article, she had arrived in Stockholm, albeit rather belatedly, to keep her promise. She had been pleased, though surprised, that Nils was still keen for her to visit.

They stopped on the way for a quick snack because Nils realised he hadn't got much food in. He'd reckoned on eating out then doing some shopping together, he'd said, mainly because he didn't know what she ate.

On their arrival at his flat on Lilla Erstagatan, he didn't even give her time to look around. He abandoned her bags in the hallway and led her into the bedroom, where Kyra thanked him several times over.

Snuggled up in his bed, Kyra felt relaxed and safe.

"I've missed you, Kyra. I hadn't realised how much until I saw you at the airport."

"Me too." She kissed his chest as she cuddled into the nook of his arm. "I'm just so sorry it's taken so long. I hadn't expected the Aliciana story to be as big as it turned out to be, and then all of those lockdowns..." She paused. "And I didn't tell you, but Mum died during the first year, which was hell to deal with. Especially with all that happened at that time."

"Why on earth didn't you tell me?"

"We all had so much going on, and when we used to speak, I just wanted to enjoy our time chatting. Anyway, I hadn't really spent as much time with her as I should have, but I'll tell you about it another time."

Nils leant down, and with his free hand, traced the shape of her face, from her eyebrows down to her lips, then bent and kissed her. "I'm sorry you had to go through that."

"It happened. Anyway, that whole time made me rethink my choices of what to do moving forward. Thanks to James—"

"Anderson?"

"Yeah, Lukas' dad. Thanks to him giving me the exclusive interview, followed by the amazing feedback I got for the article, it's given me the confidence to go freelance. It's paid off too."

"That's fantastic news. You won't be tied to one place, and I'll be able to see more of you."

"Hopefully, yes."

Kyra was relieved by his response. Even though they had

spoken regularly over the last four years, she hadn't really known what he had going on in his life. She'd never questioned him about other women and, to be honest, she really didn't care. This was now. She lay beside him and he seemed genuinely pleased.

Nils pulled away from her. "Do you want a drink? All this sex is making me thirsty." Naked, he walked out of the bedroom then shouted from the kitchen, "Lager, or wine – or something else?"

"A lager is fine."

He returned a few minutes later with two bottles of lager and climbed back into bed.

"We'll have to get up soon if you want anything else to eat."

Kyra laughed. "Seriously, we're here in bed naked and you're thinking about food."

Nils nearly choked on his lager. "Well, that's a bit rich when you made me wait for so long! Aren't you hungry?"

"Not for food."

"Are you trying to kill me, woman?"

He took Kyra's bottle of lager from her hands and put it alongside his on the bedside table.

"Come here, then."

In the end, after energetically making love again, they both fell asleep.

The next morning, while Nils put their breakfast pots away, Kyra unpacked her clothes, hanging up the one skirt she'd brought with her. The other things, which were mostly jumpers, tops and dungarees, were shoved into a drawer where Nils had made space. She'd had no idea what the weather would be like, so had mostly brought warm clothes, although it didn't seem that much cooler than the April weather she'd left in Manchester.

When she finished, she wandered around his apartment. She hadn't been able to see it properly the previous night as they'd spent most of the time in the bedroom. The building had an elegant exterior and modern interior décor, yet the layout of the apartment seemed constrained by the age of the building, which she assumed hadn't been designed for residences. What surprised her most was that by the front door, tucked into a corner of the large lounge across from the main bedroom, was the one and only bathroom. Her idea of Sweden was that of an ultra-modern country, so she'd expected an en-suite at least.

Not surprisingly, one entire wall of the lounge was dominated by a bookcase crammed full of books. Browsing through them, she found thrillers, political commentaries and memoirs, including some books Nils had written too. Some in English, some in Swedish. Kyra recognised some of the names – Stefan Ahnhem, Henning Mankell, Stieg Larsson, and the Martin Beck series by Sjöwall and Wahlöö. She knew that the last three writers had also been journalists, and wondered if maybe Nils had dreams of writing fiction. It was strange seeing some of the books she'd read in English, here in their Swedish version.

She continued looking around the space, picking up little ornaments, or things that intrigued her.

"What was this building before it became apartments?" she asked, looking across to the kitchen and smaller bedroom across the lounge.

"I've no idea. It might always have been apartments. My aunt left it to me, otherwise I'd never have been able to afford a property in this part of town and with this view."

Kyra stood gazing out of the window onto the road that led down quite an incline to the water. She opened the doors to the small balcony and looked towards the water and the buildings in the distance. "It's certainly a great view. Is that the Old Town over there?"

"No, that's Kastellholmen, a small islet. It was part of Stockholm's air defence during World War Two. Old Town is hidden by the building opposite."

"Okay. So, you'd have a great view of the Old Town if that building wasn't blocking it. Maybe you could arrange for it to disappear so you'd have an even better view." Kyra laughed.

"Mm, outside of my skill set, I'm afraid. Anyway, I thought we'd visit Old Town today. I'm sure you'll love the old buildings."

"That sounds good. I forgot to tell you. Before I came, Jess contacted me to ask if we'd go out with her and Lukas while I'm here. Do you mind? It's been so long since I last saw them."

"No, not at all. Give her a ring. Maybe we could meet them later?"

Kyra gave Jess a ring, and after a quick catch up, passed the phone over to Nils so that he and Lukas could organise where they'd meet. Although it slightly bugged her that the men needed to organise it rather than she and Jess, she had to admit it made sense, as they both knew Stockholm.

He slipped automatically into Swedish, which she loved to hear. There was something extra sexy about his voice talking in his own language. She hadn't realised Lukas spoke fluent Swedish too. Their call ended with Nils saying, "*Hejdå,*" which was one of the few words she did know. 'Bye'.

"We're meeting them in a restaurant called Chez Jolie, in Östermalm. That's where Lukas' family have an apartment, and it's one of the most upmarket parts of Stockholm, so be ready for an interesting night out."

Slightly panicked, Kyra asked, "What's that supposed to mean? Do I have to dress up?" She wasn't keen on having to wear posh outfits. Her style was her own – individual and sometimes a little quirky, which thankfully Nils had previously mentioned liking when they'd first met several years ago.

"Wear what you want – which I know you will, anyway. You

always look good, whatever you wear – or don't wear!" He gave her a quick kiss as he walked past her.

"Okay, so, are we going off to the Old Town, Herr Berg?"

Nils answered with a string of very fast Swedish, which was completely lost on her.

"Translate, please?"

"We are, and you might just find some interesting shops around the area, too. You'll love it."

"Is that what you really said?"

"Mm, that would be telling."

Half an hour later, they were wandering down Västerlång-gatan, one of the main shopping streets in Gamla stan, where Kyra stopped to gaze in shop windows every so often, much to Nils feigned annoyance. Kyra loved the fact that the streets were mostly pedestrianised. Nils also took her to the Nobel Museum on Stortorget. There, she was fascinated by the buildings around the square, mentioning how some of them looked quite Dutch in their style.

"Those two houses are often photographed by tourists, because they are so well preserved, and you're right, they were designed in a German–Dutch renaissance style. They're very pretty, aren't they?"

Kyra nodded in agreement, suggesting they take a selfie in front of the buildings.

As they wandered, Kyra's mobile rang. "I hope it's not work," Nils said.

"No, it's Jess. We're seeing her later, so I wonder what she wants?"

Kyra listened to Jess and felt her breath catch in her throat. She struggled to know what to say, and felt guilty about her pang of disappointment amid her sympathy for her friends.

"Are they okay?" Nils asked after Kyra finished the call.

"They are, but Lukas' friend Cole has been involved in a

terrible accident in Ethiopia. James is having him flown home to Manchester, so Jess and Lukas are going back there, too. So, we're not going to be seeing them tonight, which is a shame. But understandable."

"Yes. I hope his friend is okay. I was looking forward to catching up with them, too. Never mind, I'll take you out instead." Nils continued walking but then stopped suddenly and said, "I know where I'm going to take you. Come on, it's only about three minutes. Are you feeling hungry?" Without waiting for an answer, he put his arm around her and led her through the narrow streets.

They arrived at a place called Gästabud, which, from the outside, reminded Kyra of a UK pub.

Nils walked in and asked something in Swedish before they were led to a table. "I'm going to order you the traditional food of Sweden. Okay?"

"Erm, what is it?" Kyra liked most things, but warily looked around the room to see the food other people were eating. Many of the dishes looked like raw fish, which she wasn't keen on, and as for other dishes, she hadn't got a clue what they were.

"It's meatballs, mash potato and lingonberries. It's very traditional and they do a great version here. Do you want to try?" he asked.

"Okay. I'll give it a go."

Nils ordered their food and got them both a lager. When the food arrived, the meatballs and mash looked very inviting. Tentatively, Kyra tried the lingonberries. She was pleasantly surprised. "They taste a little like cranberries, but nicer. It's good. Thank you."

When they'd finished, Nils smiled at her. "You obviously were hungry, because you ate every morsel. So, do you approve of our traditional meal?"

"Yes, it's a very – homely meal!"

Later that night, after they'd wandered around the streets on the way back to Nils' apartment, they'd settled down to chat and listen to music over several glasses of wine.

"I'm so glad you came to visit," Nils had whispered before kissing her.

"Me too."

"Maybe you can stay and get used to more Swedish dishes?"

"Maybe I can."

The next night, Nils took her to visit one of the city's popular rooftop bars. As they sat cradling their cocktails, Nils said, "There's something incredibly relaxing, looking out over this city, with a glass in hand, and beside someone special."

Kyra took a quick glance to see if he was being sarcastic. He wasn't. Instead, he looked at her with a caring smile. Feeling very contented, she whispered back, "It certainly is." *I could get used to this,* she thought.

2

APRIL 2023

STOCKHOLM THEN MANCHESTER

Jess had almost reached the height of her excitement when she heard the mobile ringing. She knew Lukas had felt her flinch, but he soothed her, whispering, "They can wait."

Once they were both satisfied, Lukas left Jess to finish showering and went to find out who'd called.

She was standing in the bedroom in her underwear, about to choose her outfit for their night out with Nils and Kyra, when Lukas walked back in, his face ashen.

Something was wrong.

"What's happened?"

"It's Cole. He's been involved in a car accident, and they're flying him home."

"Oh God, Lukas. Is it bad?" She clasped Lukas in her arms, holding him close, aware of the importance of his friend.

"I don't know. It can't be good, though, if they're flying him home," he said, his voice shaky.

Jess noticed Lukas breathing more deeply than he normally would.

"Can you ring Nils and Kyra and make our apologies?" he said. "I told Sofia we'd fly home as soon as we can. I'll check flights when I've finished showering. I can't face trying to have fun when I'm constantly thinking about Cole," he said.

"I'm sure they'll understand. Don't worry."

While Lukas showered, Jess rang Kyra and explained, saying they'd hopefully see them when they got back. And, no, they didn't know how long they'd be gone.

They'd missed the only flights to Manchester that day, so Lukas considered flying to London and then arranging for a car to drive them north, because he wanted to be there with Sofia when Cole arrived. But Jess reminded him that would probably be no quicker than waiting for the early morning flight. Plus, they'd both feel fresher having had a night's sleep, she said. If he could get any.

Jess packed a bag with just a few things they'd need when they arrived. They already had other clothes in their Manchester apartment, so they could travel light, only carrying hand luggage, which would make getting through customs quicker. While she packed, Lukas rang his dad for an update on what had happened and asked him to arrange a car to meet them at the airport.

Listening to the monosyllabic conversation, Jess heard Lukas ask his dad a series of questions. From what she could glean, James appeared to only have some information but not all of it.

When he came off the phone, Lukas explained what had happened. It seemed Cole had been involved in a car crash, and although stable for now, he was seriously injured. James had organised for him to be flown to Manchester Royal Infirmary's trauma centre, because the hospitals in Ethiopia weren't as well equipped as those in the UK. Plus, it was near to Sofia, so she could visit him regularly. The hospital was on Oxford Road, a place Jess and Lukas had passed on many occasions while travelling to and from uni, when, as students, they'd lived in Fallowfield.

After a restless night and an early start followed by a two-hour flight, they were picked up at Manchester airport and driven to their apartment. Lukas couldn't wait to get to the hospital, and after dumping his bag, he gave Jess a quick kiss and walked out to go and collect Sofia. Lukas left Jess standing alone in the middle of their apartment. On his way out of the door, he mumbled something that she assumed was "I'll ring you later with an update." Jess quietly prayed that Cole would be okay. He and Lukas were like brothers. They'd met on the first day at uni, and had stuck together ever since, with Cole joining Andersson Global at the same time as Lukas. Until he'd met her, Lukas and Cole had been inseparable. Cole not being in Lukas' life was unimaginable, so she hoped his condition wouldn't be as serious as first thought, and prayed he'd be okay.

~

After emptying the bags, she stuffed them into the bottom of the wardrobe in their bedroom, and wandered into the kitchen to make herself a cup of coffee. Jess couldn't face being in the apartment alone, waiting to hear updates from Lukas. She needed to do something, so she gave Fran a ring to see if they could meet up. Fran had recently moved to Manchester to train as a midwife. Jess didn't know why she'd left Llaneirw, or if, in fact, the move was permanent or temporary. Fran had been a bit vague about what she and Kyra were doing with their mum's house. Hopeful she'd answer, Jess dialled her number. Incredibly, Fran picked up.

"Hi. Where are you?"

"Believe it or not, I'm in Manchester. You're not around, are you...or are you on a shift?"

"I wouldn't be able to answer my phone if I was on a shift! I've got the day free. How amazing is that!"

Before Fran could say anything else, Jess asked, "Do you want to meet up? I'm at the apartment, so we could meet in the Alchemist, New York Street, if you fancy it? My treat."

"Yea! Are you okay? You sound a bit shaky?"

"I'll explain when we meet."

"Okay, I'll definitely be there if it's your treat. Thanks. What time?"

"Around one. Gives me a bit of time to get freshened up. We only got in a couple of hours ago. See you soon."

Jess threw on some jeans, a jumper and her warm jacket. Manchester felt almost as wintery as Sweden, although the cold that seeped into her bones was probably due to the lack of sleep and the rush back to the UK. She always looked forward to seeing Fran. The last time they'd caught up properly was just before her dad and Anna had moved to Broad Haven. Jess had been incredibly sad that she hadn't been able to support Fran and Kyra when their mum died; social-distancing had felt particularly barbaric when it meant not being able to support friends in their time of loss. They'd spoken on the phone, texted, and even face-timed each other, but it wasn't the same.

They bumped into each other outside the Alchemist and hugged, neither of them wanting to let go. Once inside, after ordering their food, they started to chat, and over lunch, they updated each other about everything going on in their lives, including why Fran had left Llaneirw.

"I couldn't stay in that house on my own, to be honest. It was a bit creepy, and Kyra has been spending more and more time in Manchester. The house is still ours at the moment, but it's on the market. I think Kyra's going back when she's had a few weeks in Sweden with Nils."

"Is that why you decided to move to Manchester too?" Jess asked.

"Partly, but the particular training course I wanted was here.

And of course, I see Kyra – when she's around. Actually, it works well. She left the job in Liverpool, went freelance, and bought a house in Didsbury. She's paying the mortgage, and I pay her rent – which is cheaper than looking for a flat of my own. As she's always swanning off here and there these days, I have the place to myself most of the time, anyway. Plus, it means that she doesn't have to think about the security of the house, either."

"That's cool. What's she up to?"

"She's been giving lots of talks to students studying journalism, and then sometimes she goes away to work on a new story. Lukas' dad did her a great favour by giving her that interview about his grandfather. It's helped raise her profile big-time!"

"What about you? Have you had time to meet anyone, or has it been all work and no play?" Jess asked.

"No, I've not met anyone. I'm not sure I will. I'm too fussy. The course is great, though – I'm loving it. Although it's a slog, it will be well worth getting the qualifications. They always want midwives." Fran paused to take a sip of her wine. "So, have you met Kyra's *friend* Nils?" She made quote marks in the air as she said his name.

"Sadly, not yet. We should have been going out with them last night, but had to call it off after we had the call about Cole's accident. I'm looking forward to meeting him when we get back."

At that moment, Jess' mobile rang. She glanced at it. "Sorry, I'd better answer. It's Lukas. He might have some news."

3
MANCHESTER

Sofia was waiting in the downstairs entrance lobby of the apartment when Lukas arrived.

There was something different about her and it took him a while to realise – she wasn't wearing her usual amount of make-up. She still had far more than Jess wore, but Sofia's face looked almost naked, compared to normal. He could tell she'd been crying, too.

As soon as she saw him, she rushed into his arms, asking if he'd heard anything from his dad about Cole's arrival.

"No. We only got back a couple of hours ago. I dropped my stuff off at our place, along with Jess, and headed over. I'm not sure if Cole will have arrived by the time we get to the hospital or not. I did ask Dad to let me know."

"Thanks for this, Lukas. I couldn't have coped on my own. I'm so scared. I don't know how I'd manage without Cole. He does everything. He's so organised." Then, as an afterthought, she added, "And life wouldn't be the same without him."

Lukas smiled at her. Though inside, he wondered if rather than worrying about how seriously Cole had been hurt, she was more worried about him not being well enough to keep her in the style she had been living in since their marriage.

"Come on, let's get to the hospital and see how he is."

When they arrived at the trauma centre, after asking about Cole, they were shown to a waiting room. The nurse leading the way informed them that someone would come and tell them when Cole had arrived.

Nearly an hour later, a different nurse came in to say Cole was being taken straight into surgery, and would Sofia like to see her husband beforehand?

"Sofia, do you want to see Cole?" Lukas asked, as she seemed to be in a daze and hadn't appeared to notice the nurse in the room.

She nodded, and they both followed the nurse along a corridor and into the area outside of one of the operating theatres.

Cole lay on a stretcher, covered in bloody bandages, with an oxygen mask over his face. Liquids were being fed into his body via a canula, which Lukas assumed to be plasma. Cole's face looked horribly battered and bruised, and he had a nasty cut on the side of his head, but the worst visible injury was to his left leg, which seemed to be lying at a very strange angle. Of course, they had no idea of any internal injuries that he may have.

Sofia looked as though she would pass out at any minute. The nurse encouraged her to speak to Cole before they took him into surgery. Gingerly, she leant down and gently kissed his forehead, whispering, "Love you, babe."

Lukas led her back to the waiting room, and after sitting with her for a while, went off in search of coffee and biscuits. He took the opportunity to ring Jess so he could update her, too.

Jess seemed to take quite a time to answer her mobile, and when she did, she was giggling.

"Where are you?" Lukas demanded.

"I'm having lunch with Fran. I couldn't stay in the apartment all day, with my mind churning over the worst scenarios. How is Cole?"

Lukas paused before he answered. "We don't know. I'm surprised you asked."

"Don't be like that, Lukas. I know how much you love him. That's why I couldn't just wait here on my own. I needed to get out. Plus, it brought back memories of when Dad was attacked. I didn't want to be on my own thinking about it all. And now with Cole – I don't want to upset you more. So, how is he?"

"They've taken him in for surgery, though they haven't told us much, either. He looked..." Suddenly, Lukas' voice broke. "He looked so broken and so pale." Unable to speak, he stopped to catch his breath.

"Lukas, are you okay?"

He wiped away the tears that clouded his eyes. "Not really. I wish I'd brought you with me. Sofia's in a state." He paused again. "Sorry I was short with you. I just thought you'd be at home, and I hadn't thought about Danny. I'm so focused on Cole. I'm sorry." He took a long breath, trying to calm the panic that gradually built up inside him. "How is Fran?" he eventually managed.

"She's good. Got lots going on. But never mind that. Do you want me to get a taxi over to the hospital to join you?"

Lukas suddenly felt his whole body relax. He needed Jess with him. If the worse happened to Cole, he didn't think he'd cope alone, and definitely not with Sofia. "Please, that means so much."

"I'll text you when I arrive and you can let me know where you are. We've finished eating, so I can get a taxi in the next half hour. See you soon. Love you."

"Love you too."

With Jess by his side, he could keep calm and face anything.

Arriving back at Cole's room, Lukas saw that Sofia stood by the window, scrolling on her mobile phone. He glared at her. Her earlier panic seemed to have dissipated, and now she appeared to be far more interested in texting someone.

"Here's your coffee. I just phoned Jess; she's coming to join us. Have they given you any more news yet?"

Sofia glanced up, as though Lukas were interrupting something important.

"No, not yet. How long do you think they're going to be?"

"Why? Is there somewhere else you'd rather be?"

Sofia looked taken aback.

"Er, no," she said. "But it seems to be taking forever." She took a drink of the coffee Lukas had brought.

"Have you noticed how badly hurt Cole is? It isn't like he's just got a few broken ribs. He's having major surgery. He could be bleeding out on the inside, as far as we know." Lukas turned towards the door. "I'll wait in the corridor and let you know if there's any news."

His words still didn't seem to sink in.

Sofia returned to scrolling through her mobile, saying absently, "Okay. Thanks."

Lukas leant against the wall, taking deep breaths to control his growing anger. He couldn't believe how calm Sofia seemed. Maybe she was just too dumb to realise how serious Cole's injuries were.

His mobile pinged. Jess texting to say she'd arrived. When she eventually walked around the bend in the corridor, he hugged her, holding on to her as tightly as he could, trying to hold back the tears that were threatening to fall. He needed to stay strong.

A few moments later, a doctor came to tell them that Cole was out of surgery, and they'd moved him into the ICU. He'd been put in an induced coma to give his body time to heal, after all the trauma he had suffered.

They were allowed to go in to see him, as long as they were quiet and didn't stay too long.

Sofia went over to the bed and gently kissed him, taking care not to knock any of the breathing apparatus or medical equipment. When she moved away from his bed, her eyes filled with tears, and she looked the most scared Lukas had seen her all day. Weirdly, he was relieved. He had been thinking that she didn't care.

Jess put her arms around Sofia, and they stood quietly while Lukas walked over to Cole and whispered with a very unsteady voice, "Get well, mate. I need you." He touched his hand and joined the girls as they walked out of the room together.

The nurse in charge of ICU told Sofia she may as well go home and get a good rest, and then she could come back tomorrow, refreshed. She could visit at any time, though she'd be asked to leave the room if any of the medical team needed to check on Cole.

As they arrived at the lift, Sofia suddenly stopped in her tracks. "Oh my God, I've not contacted his nan. This'll kill her."

Lukas had almost forgotten Cole's nan was still alive, as he rarely talked about her. Although he knew she meant a lot to Cole because she'd brought him up after his mum had been unable to care for him. Yet somewhere along the way there seemed to be something that had broken the bond between them, though Lukas had no idea what it was.

"How is she doing, Sofia? She must be some age now," Lukas asked.

"She's in her early seventies, so not that old, but she's always been a heavy smoker and now she's got bronk—something wrong with her lungs."

"Bronchial lungs," Jess said.

"Yeah, that's it. Her smoking doesn't help, plus she's got arthritis too, so she's not finding life easy. I suppose I'd better give her a ring. I can't face driving over to Liverpool."

Lukas offered to drive her over, but Sofia obviously wasn't keen.

"You know, it might be better to wait until we know how he's doing, before you tell her."

With an expression of relief, Sofia nodded. Lukas and Jess asked if she would like to come back to their apartment, rather than be on her own, but she declined, saying that if she did sleep, she would sleep better in her own bed than any other.

4

As agreed the night before, Jess and Lukas picked up Sofia around 10.00 a.m., on their way into the hospital. On their arrival at the ICU, the doctor took Sofia aside to talk to her. She signalled for Lukas to go with her, so she wouldn't have to repeat it all to him and he'd hear the information first-hand.

After Lukas came out, he filled Jess in. Cole's prognosis wasn't good, but the decision to put him into a medical-induced coma would give time for the haematoma on his head to improve. He had also suffered some serious internal bleeding, which they'd managed to get under control, so as long as he remained stable, they weren't too worried. However, in the future, his leg would need more surgery once everything else had been sorted out.

The rest of the day – which passed incredibly slowly – they spent sitting beside Cole's bed, chatting quietly among themselves and to him, and drinking far too many cups of coffee. Jess went for some lunch with Sofia, while Lukas stayed with Cole, and when they came back, Jess returned to the cafeteria again with Lukas.

"I feel so useless. It's like living in a limbo-land, where nothing else is happening, and everything is focused on the beeps and hums of the machines in that little room," Lukas said.

He looked worn out. Jess knew he hadn't slept much the night before, but also knew there would be nothing she could say to help, but she tried anyway.

"He might know we're here. You know, they don't know what patients hear when they're in a coma. I read somewhere that some people can hear everything, whereas others don't remember a thing about it." Jess was just about to impart some more knowledge she'd learnt, when Lukas' mobile buzzed.

"It's Dad."

He answered, and after a very short conversation said, "He's just arrived. I told him to join us for a coffee, then we'll go back to Cole's room together."

James Andersson walked towards them then almost swept Jess off her feet as he first hugged her then kissed her on each cheek. After releasing her, he hugged his son in his strong embrace for quite some time.

Freeing Lukas from the hug, James asked, "You okay, son?"

Lukas nodded. His dad's presence seemed to have calmed him.

"Would you like a coffee, James?" Jess asked.

"No, I'm fine, thanks. I've not long had one. So how is Cole doing?"

Lukas gave his dad an update.

On hearing the news of Cole's condition, James looked worried. "I don't know what on earth happened out there. I've not managed to get any more information than what I shared with you the other night. It was a nightmare getting him air-lifted back here."

"Well, thank God you got him back. I don't think he'd be in such good shape if we'd left him in the hospitals out there."

"It hasn't been easy at all. I spoke to one of our local contacts, Mahmoud, and he's been in contact with Abdi's family – he was the driver. They usually have funerals twenty-four hours after someone has died in Ethiopia. I didn't know if the police would be looking into the accident and would hold things up, but it seems not. They released Abdi's body to his family straight away. Sadly, he leaves a wife and young family. Even though Abdi didn't work for us directly, I felt it only right to offer some money in terms of support. Mahmoud said they'd be grateful to receive anything."

Jess mentioned her surprise that the police hadn't looked into the accident. "Didn't they want to know what happened?"

"Generally, if it's out in the country, they just don't have the resources to follow up with everything. To be honest, the fact that we arranged to get Cole out of the country was probably quite a relief for them," James said. "Anyway, let's go and see how he's doing."

James had met Sofia many times when Lukas and Cole had been studying, so there was no formality in their greeting, and as with Jess and Lukas, he hugged her too, giving her words of comfort as he did so.

He then sat with Sofia for a short time, and despite knowing that Cole may not hear, he spoke to him as though he were involved in the conversation. Jess smiled to herself. James clearly shared her hopes about familiar voices. The more Cole heard, the better the chances of his recovery.

Over the following two weeks, Jess and Lukas took it in turns to go to the hospital to sit with Sofia, and they'd stay with Cole while she went to get something to eat.

The days seemed to drag on and Jess knew Lukas found it harder and harder to hang around in the hospital. It wasn't that he didn't care, he'd told her. He just felt annoyed by his inability to do anything useful. He found the interminable hours of waiting around were the worst.

At the beginning of the third week, the doctor told Sofia they were going to remove Cole's breathing apparatus, to see if he could breathe on his own. The doctor signalled for the nurse to help him remove the ventilator and other medical paraphernalia.

Sofia stood in the corner of the room, clearly terrified that Cole would stop breathing altogether. Jess moved closer to her, holding her hand in support. She, too, prayed that Cole would breathe for himself.

"I don't think I can stay to watch," Sofia said, turning to walk out.

"Come on, Sofia." Jess grabbed her hand tighter. "If he wakes up, you want him to see your face, don't you?"

Sofia nodded, but Jess could still see the terror in her eyes.

The medical staff removed the ventilator and all the apparatus that went with it. To everyone's relief, Cole started to breathe on his own.

When the staff walked out of the room, the doctor said, "Don't panic that he's not come around yet. It's early days, and there is plenty of time for that to happen. His body will be settling and healing itself. Keep talking to him as much as you can. Hearing your voice will be a huge help."

Tentatively, Sofia walked over to the bed and gently kissed Cole on his lips.

"Wake up, babes. I want to see your lovely green eyes."

Following the doctor's suggestions, she continued talking to him, and she played some of the songs from her playlist on her mobile – ones she knew he loved.

A few days later, when Lukas rather than Jess was visiting, Cole opened his eyes.

5
MAY 2023
MANCHESTER

Hesitantly, he opened his eyes and, for a while, thought he'd gone blind. He began to see shapes but then he perceived that he had a thin layer of gauze in front of his eyes – everything was blurred. He blinked, trying to clear his vision, and heard someone shout, "Nurse, he's awake. My husband is awake."

Sofia!

He tried to move, but the nurse who had hurriedly arrived at his bedside told him to stay still. She held his wrist and checked his pulse then shone a light in his eyes, which was even more annoying than the blurriness. He tried to move his head away, though it hurt like hell.

"That's a good sign," she said. "Come and speak to your husband for a little while. Be gentle, and try not to excite him in any way."

He shut his eyes then opened them again to see Sofia's beautiful face emerge from the blur. When he tried to speak, she didn't even hear him.

"Don't worry, I'm here, babe. I've been so scared. But you're going to be okay. They've said you may have some problems with your leg, and your memory might be a little scrambled, but you're here and you're alive."

She bent down towards him and gingerly kissed his cheek, obviously scared of hurting him.

Again, he tried to speak, and managed to whisper, "Sofia. I thought I was dead. I didn't think I would see you again."

At that moment, someone moved nearer the bed and, touching his hand, said, "Cole, mate, I'm so relieved you're okay."

Cole smiled up at him, wondering if he should know him. He glanced up at Sofia, who didn't help. He panicked. This guy certainly knew him. This was going to be harder than he thought.

The blond man looked at Sofia. "He doesn't seem to recognise me."

Sofia came nearer the bed again and looked down at Cole. "Babe, it's Lukas. Don't you recognise him? You can't have forgotten your best friend. He's been here nearly every day to check up on you."

Cole smiled up at Lukas. "Thanks, mate. My memory is playing tricks."

"No worries. Now that I've seen you're conscious and normal – well, fairly normal, I'll leave you two in peace. See you later. I'll bring Jess next time too."

Sofia kissed Cole again, saying, "I'm just going to say bye to Lukas. I'll be back."

Sofia walked over to the door with Lukas, who seemed to be pondering something. "You okay, Lukas?"

"I'm a bit shaken that he didn't recognise me. Have the doctor's said anything about him having memory loss?"

"Not much, only that it is quite likely he'll have forgotten some things, especially with the head injury he had, and the loss of blood. It might take some time but I'm sure he'll soon be back to normal. Thanks for coming and being here with me. I'd never have coped on my own." She leant in and kissed Lukas before returning to Cole's bedside.

Cole made great improvement over the few days following his awakening. Even the doctors were surprised about the speed of his recovery.

A few days later, they moved Cole out of ICU into a private room. And by the end of the week, they allowed him out of bed, but only if he used a wheelchair, because the doctors didn't want him putting any weight on his leg, which still required surgery.

Whenever Sofia visited, Cole always seemed relieved when it was her alone. He seemed particularly keen to ask her to talk to him about things they'd done over the last year, and who their friends were. He wanted her help to bring his memory back. She was more than happy to waffle on about their friends, where they'd travelled to, and the holidays they'd previously taken.

"I'll show you all the photos when you come home and you're less tired."

~

Lukas returned for a visit with Jess. Cole should have remembered her, as they'd all studied in Manchester at the same time, but now she seemed like a stranger to him.

"Have you remembered who I am today?" Lukas asked as soon as he came into the room.

"Yes, I remember you from the other day. I've not got short memory problems, just long-term ones. Thanks for coming again, and as promised, you've brought Jess."

Jess gave Cole a kiss and then went over to talk to Sofia, to ask how things were going.

Cole was sitting up in bed now, looking much brighter than the last time Lukas had visited.

"So, I bet you can't wait to get back to watch a City game, can you?"

After a slight pause, Cole answered. "Why did you ask me that, when you know I hate footie?"

"You haven't forgotten that then! Do you remember anything about the accident?" Lukas asked.

Cole remained quiet for a time, as if trying to recall what had happened.

"No, I've been told that I was travelling in a jeep. I think I must have been on the way to my hotel. Then I have some vague memories of someone helping me after we'd crashed, then after that I only see flashes and remember strange sounds. Then I woke up here." He looked over at Lukas. "Do you have any more information?"

"Sadly, not much. The driver died instantly when the jeep hit the tree. In fact, you were lucky you were thrown from the jeep, otherwise you might have been dead too. Do you even remember why you were in Africa?"

"Sofia told me. I remembered a few bits when she talked about it, but again, not much. I'm sorry I just seem to have a blank where my brain used to be."

Lukas laughed. "What brain? Did you actually have one before?" He smiled at Cole, who returned his smile.

Jess wandered over and told Lukas they should get going, as they'd got some things to organise, plus they shouldn't tire Cole out too much

After saying their goodbyes, they set off for the car park.

Walking back to their car, Jess could tell something was bothering Lukas.

"What's up? You're far too quiet. I thought you'd be pleased to see how well Cole is doing."

"Mm. I am, but didn't he seem 'off' to you?"

"Well, yes, but he has been in a major accident. I think even you'd feel a bit 'off'. It's probably just the concussion affecting his memory, and he's going to feel very strange after being put in a coma then waking up to find out he doesn't know things. He's very lucky to be alive from what I heard you say about the accident."

Lukas put his arm around her, and kissing her, said, "Thank you. You're making complete sense. I supposed I expected to see my old pal back, and he isn't yet. I'm being selfish, but I've missed him."

"I know. He'll be back soon. Wait and see. Come on, we'd better go and get the stuff we promised your mum."

When they'd finished shopping, on the way to see Lukas' parents, it was Jess' turn to be quiet. She'd never really gelled with Sofia. Her complete opposite. It seemed to Jess that all she ever thought about were her clothes, money, and her 'lifestyle'. And she loved posting her images on social media. Jess wondered if Sofia really wanted to become an influencer for some clothing company. After all, she was always buying new outfits, even though she had a wardrobe crammed with clothes. And she never just walked into a room, she sashayed like a model wanting to be noticed by everyone. The exact opposite of Cole's quiet confidence, unassuming manner and incredible intelligence. Jess had often wondered what he saw in Sofia, although she suspected she knew exactly what she saw in him. Money!

Although this was perhaps an uncharitable thought, she knew that deep down, Lukas agreed. Thinking about it, she'd never seen him engage in a long conversation with Sofia, either.

Today, seeing her with Cole in the hospital, Jess recognised that Sofia's 'perfect' world had suddenly come to a halt.

6

Propped up, Cole watched Sofia's every move as she walked around his bed, with her willowy, modelesque elegance. He watched her as though he'd never seen her before, and she were the most beautiful woman in the world. Which in fact she was. All he'd seen for the last month were mundane hospital rooms and people dressed in scrubs or uniforms. He'd seen so many medical practitioners over the time, he kept forgetting who was who. But Sofia wafted a breath of fresh air into the room every day.

She gave him a glorious smile. "How are you feeling today, babe?"

"Much better, especially for seeing you." He smiled but then winced, as one of the cuts on his face pulled sharply.

His smile completely disappeared when the nurse who he called 'The Vampire' entered the room.

"Meet Madam Dracula."

A lady carrying a small box had entered the room without any noise and surprised Sofia by her sudden appearance.

"I've come to take more of his blood," the nurse said.

"Ah, I get the bad joke now." Sofia smiled.

"You wouldn't if you were on the receiving end of her needles. I'm lucky I've got any blood left." Cole winced again, but this time as the nurse started to take blood from his arm.

"You know it's all in a good cause. It helps us see how you're getting on."

She finished and disappeared as silently as she'd arrived.

Cole smiled as he noticed Sofia's surprise at the nurse's quiet departure. *Maybe she is a vampire after all!*

Sofia sat back next to his bed, holding his hand, and started to tell him more about what had been going on over the last two weeks. She suddenly stopped halfway through a sentence.

"Oh, God. I still haven't told your nan. I didn't tell her you were in here to start with. I didn't want to upset her too much, you know, with her asthma and things...But I ought to let her know now that you're on the mend."

Cole looked slightly panicked. "Don't you think I should, babe?"

"Er, no. Maybe not yet. Let's wait until I'm out of hospital and we'll go over to see her, and we can talk to her all about it then. What she doesn't know won't hurt her, will it? If we tell her now, it might make her ill. Does that sound fair?"

"Okay, if you think she won't worry." Sofia, although relieved, also felt a little surprised.

"I don't talk to her that often, you know that. She won't even wonder why I've not called. She knows I often go away for work, so she probably hasn't even noticed that I haven't been in touch. I think that's much better for her health, don't you?"

Sofia nodded.

They were interrupted for a second time when Cole's doctor came into his room to talk to them about operating on Cole's left leg. It needed some realigning; the break hadn't been clean. The operation would correct the bone alignment, although they would probably have to add some metal rods to help. Without it, his leg wouldn't heal completely and he might have a permanent limp. He added that they were very pleased with Cole's overall recovery and thought that now he'd be well enough to cope with the operation.

Sofia was pleased. She didn't really fancy the idea of being married to someone with a limp; she wanted to see Cole walking normally again. She knew it was a mean thing to think, but she didn't see herself as someone living with an invalid.

The next morning, Sofia dropped into the hospital before the nurses gave Cole his meds for the operation. He kissed her before telling her to go shopping or do something to cheer herself up. She didn't need to be told twice. She checked with the nurse what time Cole would be back and conscious, then set off into town.

She'd made the most of the time to herself. She'd had her nails done; bought herself a new dress and some shoes that she'd had her eye on for a couple of weeks. And afterwards, leaving all of her purchases in the boot of her car, she went back to see Cole and was pleased to see him back in his room, wide awake. The operation had gone well.

Sofia looked forward to getting him home and getting away from the smell of the hospital. Her life had come to a complete standstill since the accident. She looked forward to getting their old life back again.

~

Cole was allowed home with crutches a few days after his leg operation. He'd completely recovered and had healed from the other medical injuries he'd suffered in the accident, so as long as he took care with his leg, the doctors thought he would do better at home rather than stay in hospital any longer. He and Sofia had been given explicit instructions that he should take great care not to walk on his leg for too long and that he shouldn't bump it on anything. Sofia made the decision that once home, she'd sleep in the spare room. She was terrified she'd kick his leg in her sleep.

The first few days, Cole didn't get up until later in the day. He still seemed to have some of the drugs in his system, which meant he often became sluggish and slept more than usual. During the second week, though, he began getting up at a more normal time and joined Sofia for breakfast.

"I need to go into town this morning, babes, to get some food. Will you be okay on your own?" Sofia asked.

"I've only got a bad leg. I can amuse myself quite easily." He smiled at her. "You don't need to worry so much. I'm on the mend and I feel so much better. Go on, get out and visit the shops."

A little later, Sofia left. While she shopped, Cole took the opportunity to look around the flat. He wanted to reacclimatise himself to its layout and find some of his paperwork. He hobbled around the flat, becoming more adept with his crutches as he went.

Eventually, he went into his study and started rifling through the drawers. He soon managed to find what he was searching for. His bank accounts, other important paperwork, and a personal injury insurance that had been set up when he started working at Andersson Global. He took the paperwork into the other room to read through. His office chair was less comfortable than the sofa and he still needed to rest his leg.

After reading through some other things, he began to come to some decisions that he knew Sofia would be surprised about, but decisions he nevertheless had to make.

When she walked back into the apartment, Sofia dumped the

food shopping on the kitchen island and walked over to Cole to kiss him.

"What've you been up to while I was out?"

Trying not to look guilty, because he knew she'd probably nag him for moving around too much, he answered, "I just went through some of my papers, insurance and stuff like that. Wanted to see if my memory would get a jolt looking through them."

"And did it?"

"Some, but at least I've made some decisions."

"O-kay...Good or bad decisions?"

"Depends how you see things."

Sofia looked at him quizzically. "Come on, don't mess about. What plans are you making for us? I need to know too."

"Well, I've decided I probably won't go back to work. I..."

Sofia looked shocked. "What do you mean, you're not going back to work? How are we going to afford this place?"

"Don't panic, Sofia. I've got insurance cover and I'll get a good handout after the accident, especially if I claim on the company's policy. We'll be fine when it comes to money, you needn't worry."

"But what are you going to do? Surely, you're not going to stay at home all day?"

"I don't know yet, but, there will be something. I'd better get in touch with James to tell him I'm not going back."

Sofia stayed quiet for a long time, seeming to think through what it would mean in reality. Eventually, she said, "You do realise, when you get that insurance money, you'd better put it somewhere safe, otherwise you know me, I'll be dipping in it to go shopping. Although, we could go on a decent holiday together and have a real relax?"

"I hope you're not going to be able to spend the amount I should get as an insurance pay-out. It should pay off the rest of the mortgage on this flat, and then some." He grabbed her hand and pulled her down onto the sofa next to him. "A holiday in the sun would be good. We can do that too." He kissed her passionately and felt Sofia relaxing into his embrace.

Cole's kisses were good, but his kisses now had far more urgency to them. She could feel herself melting to his touch as he moved his lips down her neck. Groaning, she pushed him away.

"Come on, babes, stop getting me excited. You're still recovering. I can't get you too excited, it's not good for you." She leapt up off the sofa. "I'll make us some coffee."

Now it was Cole's turn to groan. "You can't do that to me. Don't I deserve a little more of your loving?" He laughed.

"Maybe when I won't be terrified of kicking you in the middle of my passion."

She went into the kitchen area, put the coffee machine on, and started putting the food away, trying to calm herself.

Taking Cole's coffee over to him, she said, "You know Lukas and Jess want to spend some time with us, if you feel up to it. He was incredibly upset when we got the news about your accident. And he's been such a good friend, visiting you, looking after me. What do you think?"

"I'd rather just spend more time with you than be with anyone else, just until I feel a hundred percent. Do you mind?"

"No, I love being with you. Anyway, I know they'd talked about joining Nils and Kyra in Sweden for Midsummer celebrations. Should I tell them we'll see them when they get back?"

Cole nodded, already engrossed in a magazine article he'd just started to read.

"Cole—"

He raised his eyes with a *what's-up-now?* look.

"Now you're beginning to recover, are you going to get in

touch with your nan? We could go over to see her together. I've not seen her for ages."

"No, I'd rather wait until I'm one hundred percent – I'd rather she doesn't know about the accident altogether. I don't want to cause her to be ill because of me. We'll get in touch soon, though, I promise." He turned back to his magazine and continued to read the article he'd been engrossed in.

"Okay," she said, surprised that Cole still didn't want to see his nan, when she was the only family that he had contact with. Wondering about the reasons why he really didn't want to see her, she began tidying the kitchen.

7
JUNE 2023
STOCKHOLM

"Kyra, I've just tripped over your DMs." Nils stood in front of her, his hands on his hips.

Without glancing up from her computer, where she was busy finishing some work, she muttered, "Sorry," and continued typing.

"Come on, you know we need to keep the space tidy. It's not a huge flat, and when we're both here, it's even smaller. I don't expect to find your stuff in the middle of the floor."

Kyra stopped typing, and standing up, stretched up to kiss Nils. He ducked out of her grasp. "No, you're not getting out of it that way. I'm serious."

"Come on, Nils. It's not the end of the world. Stop being such a neat freak!" She laughed and tried to catch him again.

After some grumbling, he gave in, allowing her to capture him, and accepted her embrace and kisses.

"I'm sorry. I just like to be tidy. I've lived on my own for so long, I'm not used to having someone else's stuff around the place."

"We've been together for several months. I'd have thought you'd be used to me by now. I'll never be as neat as you, but I am trying." Kyra tried to console him with more kisses, which this time, he wasn't evading. "Let me just finish this last few paragraphs and I'll move anything that offends your eyes."

Nils muttered something in Swedish and stomped off to make some coffee. She could hear him in the kitchen, beginning to laugh. Kyra began to wonder if she could ever live with him full time if he would always be so obsessive about neatness. She wasn't an unclean person, but neither was she as tidy as Nils. And she did have to remind herself, that his flat, although not that small, didn't have lots of storage space.

She recalled the run they'd been on earlier that morning: the air, clear and crisp and the views across the river to Old Town, beautiful. Whether she wanted to admit it to herself or not, the more time they spent together – making love, going out walking, chatting, or purely relaxing together – the more she knew she wanted this to last.

On cue, just as the coffee was ready, she closed her laptop, having finished the article. Nils sat next to her on the sofa.

"Hey, did I tell you that Lukas gave me a ring the other day?" he said.

"Oh, I didn't know you knew him that well?"

"What, you mean well enough for him to phone me? I know you know Jess better than me, but we are allowed to talk." Nils laughed. "He wants us to celebrate Midsummer with them. It's 21st of this month."

"Yeah, I sort of know when it is, but I didn't know you'd celebrate Midsummer. I don't see you as a hippy," Kyra said.

"What do you mean, a hippy?"

"Well, I see it as a bit of a hippy-type celebration. You know, in the UK, there are always lots of people who turn up at Stonehenge and other places, along with Druids. You know, all very alternative. I'm not really into that sort of stuff." Kyra laughed.

"Well, it's nothing to do with hippies here. Like everywhere, it's the longest day of the year, but as we have such long winters, we enjoy celebrating the extra-long day. It's a huge tradition which is second only to Christmas. Most of us own holiday homes on one of the islands in the Stockholm archipelago and I'd planned to take you to mine, but Lukas has invited us to theirs, which is quite a bit grander. What do you think?"

"Well, I would like to have seen your holiday home, but since we missed seeing Lukas and Jess when I first came over, it will be good to see them both. Yeah, I think it's a great idea."

Nils kissed her. "I'm glad. I'll let Lukas know. By the way, have you heard how his friend is doing? He didn't mention anything when I spoke to him."

"Oh. Jess says he's on the mend and came out of hospital recently. From what she said, I got the impression that Lukas was pretty pissed that Cole hasn't wanted to see him that much. He wants to spend his time with Sofia at the moment."

"Why's he so annoyed?"

"They were best buddies at college, and they confided in each other all the time. I don't think Lukas can grasp the idea that Sofia wants Cole to herself, after nearly losing him."

Nils nodded. "I suppose. Oh well, hopefully Lukas will be able to relax while he's here. He says they'll be arriving at the end of next week, which will give us a little time to get things organised for the trip."

"What do we have to organise? Do we need to do some cooking or anything?" Kyra asked.

"I'll check with Lukas. He may have already arranged to have food delivered to his place. It gets pretty busy during the celebrations, with everyone baking and preparing. Knowing him, he'll have arranged for someone to deliver food already."

"Wow, that is organised."

"Well, I know Jess doesn't like cooking, and I'm not sure how much Lukas will do, either. The main thing is, we'll all have a lot of fun. Oh, and he told me to say, he's booked us tickets to travel on the Cinderella ferry, which is about two hours long, but takes a great trip around the Stockholm archipelago, so you'll see lots of the other islands on the way."

"That's thoughtful of him. I really fancy that. I've been intrigued to know what the other parts of Stockholm look like – outside the city."

During her time in Stockholm, Nils had taken her to see quite a lot of the popular tourist sights, but more excitingly, he'd also taken her to favourite places of his. The one she loved best was Tantolunden, an area in his neighbourhood of Södermalm. A beautiful park where they'd wandered together one afternoon, along the winding pathways, before stopping to sit under the trees, looking out across to Årsta holmar, a tiny islet and one of the many islands that make up Stockholm. Kyra thought it quite magical. Everywhere she looked, something fascinating caught her eye. Flowers, trees, and the occasional small cottage. One place she definitely looked forward to revisiting.

Two weeks later, two days before Midsummer, Kyra and Nils went to meet Jess and Lukas at Strandvägen for the ferry to the island, where they would disembark at Sandhamn, the main village and harbour. Unsurprisingly, considering the time of year and the importance of the Midsummer celebrations, the boat was packed. Despite the crowds, Kyra was grateful to Lukas for giving her the opportunity to see so much of the countryside she would otherwise have missed. The small towns, hundreds of rocky, forested islands and many, many sailing ships and vessels along the way.

They arrived around 12.30, just in time for lunch, so Lukas led the way to a local restaurant called 'Ankaret'. It seemed that knowing the locals was a great advantage, and even though there were many tourists and other people queuing, as soon as the owner saw Lukas, she greeted him like a friend. He ordered for everyone, while Jess, Nils and Kyra sat outside in a spot where they could watch the boats coming and going in the harbour. Lukas soon arrived back with iced coffee, sandwiches and cinnamon biscuits.

"We'll be eating enough food over the next few days, so I thought a snack would be okay for now."

"It's great, thanks, Lukas. I'm just enjoying how beautiful it is here," Kyra said, completely in her element, lapping up the sun. "I can't wait to see your house. How long has your family owned it?"

"It was in my mum's family, and they gave it as a wedding present to Mum and Dad when they were first married. They wanted somewhere they could come to in the summer. They've done a lot to it over the years. Once we've finished eating, we'll walk there. It's not far."

As promised, when they'd finished their lunch, with Lukas leading the way, the four of them wandered through the streets, having to stop every so often to ensure they hadn't lost Kyra, still busy taking in the sights as she went. Captivated by how close the buildings were to each other, she saw that in some places only a small pathway ran between them. Many of the houses were wooden and several of them had balconies on the first floor, giving views of the sea. Some even had little turrets. The various designs held a magical feel to them, helped by the fact most of them were painted in different hues of red or yellow.

They walked until they were a little way out of the centre, where the main glut of houses stood, then, set in between some tall pine trees, stood a detached, wooden house painted a deep ochre.

"It's beautiful, Lukas." Kyra couldn't stop smiling.

Telling her to leave her bag and placing her own by the gate too, Jess took Kyra's hand and led her through the garden gate. Exchanging a look of exasperation, Lukas and Nils picked up the girls' bags and followed them.

At the front of the house, there was a small veranda with two chairs. At the back where the house faced the sea, yet another veranda led onto a small patio where a table and chairs stood. Planters surrounded the patio, filled with beautiful shrubs, having the effect of softening the harder stones.

"Can you imagine us eating out here? It's a glorious place to be, and especially when the nights are so long," Jess enthused, leading Kyra into the house. "Come and see what you think."

Grooved wood covered much many of the walls inside the house, painted a pale grey. The stairs, also wooden, were not carpeted. In fact, none of the rooms had fitted carpets, only large rugs. The style was generally simple, yet in places a complete contradiction, particularly when it came to some of the light fittings. To Kyra's surprise, one of two rooms was lit by stunningly ornate small chandeliers. The bedrooms were all wallpapered, in beautiful pastel colours and patterns, with matching pillows on the beds. From upstairs, there were wonderful views of the sea, particularly from the room with the small balcony. This was the room Lukas had given to her and Nils. She did wonder, though, how cold the house must feel during the winter. Jess told her that quite a lot of the older people went to live in the city during the winter months, because of the dark and the cold. Also, there were no cars to get around and the facilities were poor. Though it certainly was perfect for a summer break to get away from the hustle and bustle of urban life, and Kyra thought it magical.

While Jess showed Kyra around, Lukas and Nils had grabbed some beers from the fridge, and by the time the girls had finished the tour, they found them both relaxing in the sun.

"Who looks after the house when your family aren't here?" Nils asked.

"Lars, our neighbour. He's always lived here, even during the winter. He and his wife stock the fridge up for us and make sure the house is aired before we come over. Dad pays them a retainer to do that. They're brilliant. I know that Ebba will have bought all of the things we need for our Midsummer celebration, plus, I bet she's made us a cake too."

"It's such a pretty house. Did your mum choose all the decoration, Lukas?" Kyra asked.

Jess answered for him. "Karin's an interior designer. She's quite well-known in Sweden."

"You didn't tell me that, Nils," Kyra said.

"You didn't ask," he replied.

"Typical man's reply!"

Turning to Lukas, Kyra said, "You're very lucky."

"He knows," Jess said. "I keep reminding him that not many of us have the luxury that comes with money."

Kyra noticed Lukas give her a sideways look, which Jess also caught.

"I sometimes find it hard to accept that being with Lukas means that things get done, that if I wasn't with him, wouldn't. I like to keep his feet firmly on the ground. It's too easy to expect things when money comes easily."

"I'm not going to be allowed to forget," Lukas said, giving Jess a gentle shove. "Changing the subject, does anyone fancy a little dip before we make tonight's dinner?"

"Try to stop me," Nils said, already starting to remove his clothes.

"Erm, not me, thanks. I prefer my sea nice and warm," Kyra said.

"I'm happy to stay here too. I'm not sure that the water is

that warm yet. We'll just drink a few more glasses of wine while we wait."

Jess disappeared into the house to get another bottle.

When she returned, Kyra asked her if Lukas' parents would be joining them for Midsummer.

"No, his sister Charlott has a new boyfriend and she wants to take him home to meet them. I think she's quite serious about him."

"Do you get on well with his parents?"

"Yes. They're lovely and incredibly supportive. Considering it was down to me that Lukas' great-grandfather was outed for his part in the sinking of the Aliciana, they're very generous to me. Both of his parents are easy to get on with too, and it's great having them so near to us when we're home in Manchester, especially when my dad and Anna are in Spain."

Nils and Lukas, both dripping wet, ran out of the sea and aimed straight for Kyra and Jess, who ended their quiet conversation abruptly.

"Don't think you're coming near me," Jess said to Lukas before running into the house to escape him. He ran after her, and Kyra and Nils could hear screams and giggling coming from inside, eventually followed by silence.

Nils plonked his wet body onto the seat Jess had just evacuated.

"You needn't try that, either," Kyra said.

"I don't need an excuse to get you naked," he said, winking at her. "Why don't you come and join me in the water? It isn't that cold. You'll soon get used to it and I can easily keep you warm."

Kyra was going to say no, but the sight of his strong, glistening body removed any negative thoughts, and after putting her hair up in the scrunchy she always had handy, she stripped off her dungarees and underwear, and taking his hand, followed him into the water.

8

JUNE 2023, MIDSUMMER
SANDHAMN

Everyone got up early for another swim in the cool water before a substantial breakfast, which they ate out on the patio, while listening to the gentle lapping of the sea. For the rest of the morning, they sat around chatting and drinking coffee and the odd beer. Lukas had warned them that when it came to the afternoon celebrations, they'd probably do a lot of walking.

They moved into the front garden early afternoon and continued to chat until their conversation was interrupted by music that appeared to be getting closer by the second. Eventually a small farm vehicle adorned with leaves and greenery appeared around the corner. On the back sat a group of musicians; one played an accordion and the other two accompanied him with the guitar and drums. A small procession of locals dressed in national costume followed behind the vehicle. Most of the women and young girls wore garlands of flowers on their heads and to Kyra the whole scene evoked a feeling of nostalgia, but also one of celebration and joy.

As the vehicle came past their house, with Lukas taking the lead, they all followed on behind the procession. Everyone was in high spirits, with the crowd of followers growing as they made their way to the centre of Sandhamn.

The harbour was filled with a wide variety of vessels, large and small, all decorated with Swedish flags flapping in the breeze.

Everyone they met welcomed them, inviting them to join in their celebrations. The four of them spent the afternoon listening to the local musicians, watching the dancing and then the games that the younger children were involved in. And of course, drinking far too much schnapps and beer.

Around 4.00 p.m., Lukas suggested they all go back and enjoy the feast that Ebba had prepared. All the girls had to do was take the food out of the fridge and put out the dishes and cutlery for serving and eating.

Kyra had helped Jess take the food out into the garden, where they'd sat around the table they'd eaten breakfast at earlier.

The food looked and tasted amazing. Kyra had no idea what to expect, but it seemed that the food served at Midsummer was fairly traditional. There was pickled herring with a variety of sauces, including horseradish and mustard, Swedish cured salmon, seeded crispbread, and boiled new potatoes with fresh dill, soured cream and chives. Alongside these dishes, a whole salmon, which was followed by Ebba's famous Midsummer strawberry cake. Kyra remembered how on the journey over to Sandhamn, Jess had told her all about the cake she'd eaten at her first Midsummer the year before. Ebba's cake certainly looked too beautiful to eat. What could have been seen as a simple sponge cake was elevated by the cream covering, which included roasted chopped nuts, almonds and also a few small meringues, topped with fresh strawberries.

Kyra didn't think she'd be able to eat for at least a week!

Happy and full of a wonderful feast, she sat with her friends in the light of the longest day, getting merrier by the minute. They drank schnapps and shared stories, warmed by the small fire Lukas had lit.

"I don't think I ever want this day to end," Kyra just about managed to say, very slightly slurring her words.

"Yes, it's been a wonderful day. Thank you both," Nils said to Jess and Lukas.

"I feel more relaxed than I have for weeks, thanks to you guys," Lukas replied. "I've been so disorientated by what's been happening with Cole, I haven't given myself any downtime, so this has been great for me. Thank you."

Nils leant over and gripped Lukas' hand in acknowledgement. Then, apparently wanting to lighten the moment, he leapt up, saying, "So who's up for a skinny dip?"

Jess shook her head. "Not tonight. I'm too tired, plus I need to clear these dishes into the house. But you two can, even if we go to bed."

"I'll help you," Lukas offered.

Without a word, Nils just raised his eyebrows to ask Kyra.

"Maybe, as long as you promise not to let me drown. I think I've probably drunk quite a lot."

"I'm a Viking. I'll protect you." As he spoke, he was already stripping off his clothes, then he lifted Kyra out of her seat and carried her to the water's edge, threatening to throw her in fully clothed. She managed to wriggle out of his grasp, and quickly pulled her clothes off before jumping into the water after him.

The next morning, the house remained very quiet, and even breakfast was a gentle affair, with everyone trying hard not to clink dishes together or make any sudden loud noises.

Later, when their heads and stomachs had settled down, Lukas took them out onto the water in his family's small boat. It was interesting seeing this side of the island from the water, and fascinating passing the variety of houses that sat hiding among the trees.

Later, for their meal, they finished off the leftovers of the food from the night before, and after drinking far less alcohol, went to bed at a fairly normal time, so they'd be ready to leave early the next morning.

Kyra didn't want to leave. She'd enjoyed this trip and had particularly loved being part of a couple with Nils and spending time with Jess and Lukas. She could have spent much longer relaxing in the beautiful house by the water.

9
JUNE 2023
MANCHESTER

After the wonderful long weekend on Sandhamn, Kyra flew back to Manchester. Although she'd finished writing an article for the council several months earlier, it still needed to be signed off. The council members who'd been prevaricating over certain aspects of the report had at last given their consent, which meant she could go ahead and get the article printed. She'd been happy to go with their schedule. It wasn't something that would make much difference to her, as they'd already paid a good sum for her time and the finished article.

Knowing she didn't have to send the work until the next day, Kyra took the opportunity to get some food in and tidy up ready for Nils' upcoming visit.

She loved her little house, which wasn't actually that little. During the pandemic, she hadn't needed to travel so much, and had done quite a lot of her work from home. She'd saved on travel expenses and all the other things that went along with meeting up with clients and friends. By the time the country had opened up again, she had a pretty good savings pot, which, alongside the money she had from the sale of her Liverpool flat, helped her to get a mortgage for her first house. When the sale of her mum's house went through, she'd have half the money from that sale, with the other half going to Fran. They'd also been left money when their father died. At the age of thirty-three, she was very proud to have her own house, though she wished it hadn't been in such sad circumstances.

She wondered what Nils would think of her house. His apartment and her building were like chalk and cheese. Her Victorian terrace, which had been beautifully modernised by previous owners, stood in a quiet, leafy street in Didsbury, a suburban village outside Manchester, which certainly wasn't a metropolis like Stockholm. Although, in the village centre, there were plenty of good restaurants and bars, and it only took around twelve minutes by train to Manchester centre, and around thirty minutes to drive. Didsbury felt cosier than Stockholm, but it didn't have the amazingly crisp, clear air. She hoped Nils would like her home as much as she liked his.

When she'd arrived back from Sweden, she didn't know if Fran would be home or not, but either way, they'd catch up soon. She looked forward to introducing her to Nils, certain that Fran would like him.

As she moved around the kitchen, putting away the food she'd bought, she listened to music through her earbuds, often dancing between cupboards. She hadn't heard Fran arrive and nearly jumped out of her skin when she turned around and saw her sister standing behind her, a bemused smile on her face.

"You'll give me a heart attack one of these days." She took the earbuds out and hugged Fran.

"How was your flight?"

Kyra nodded, *Okay.*

"I'm in early again tomorrow, but we can catch up over dinner – if you haven't got plans." Fran said the last bit looking around, as if expecting someone else to be there.

"Oh, no, it's just me. Nils isn't coming until next week. I'll just take this stuff upstairs, then I'll start dinner."

They each saw to their own chores and then met back in the kitchen.

Kyra had started cooking and had already opened a bottle of red wine.

"Do you want a glass?" she asked Fran.

"Er, no, not tonight. I've got to be up early, and I don't trust myself to stick to just one. But you go ahead."

Half an hour later, they sat down to a stir-fry with mushrooms, chicken, ginger, garlic, spices and noodles. Over the meal, Kyra caught Fran up on Cole's recovery and her visit to the Midsummer celebrations in Stockholm. Then Kyra heard all about Fran's latest training mishaps and successes.

"When are you giving that talk at the journalists' conference?" Fran asked.

"The week after next. That's why Nils is coming over, so he can come with me. It's not my first talk, but it will be my biggest audience so far, so I'm a little nervous. Although, I'm hoping to persuade Nils to be involved too, when I talk about him helping out with the research in Sweden for the Aliciana story. I think I can cope with him being there."

"Mm, unless he totally puts you off."

"Why on earth should he?"

"Doesn't he think he's better than you? I mean, he's older than you and has been working in the industry a few years longer," Fran said.

"You are so distrusting of men. Just because you've had bad experiences with complete macho control-freaks doesn't mean all men are like that. There are some good ones out there."

"And they're not all lovely and treat women equally. Nils must have some bad points. You can't tell me he's perfect."

"No, I can't." Kyra smiled to herself. "His worst trait is, he's super-neat. A neat freak in fact, so I have to be on my best behaviour when I'm staying at his and not clutter up the space."

"Ha! So, he's not perfect." Fran laughed.

"Apart from that, I'd say he's a good nine," Kyra answered. "Anyway, you'll see for yourself, if you're around over the next few weeks. Er, I'm going to take him over to Llaneirw when I go to the estate agents and solicitors. Do you mind?"

"No. Why should I? The quicker we can get the house sold the better and then we can get on with our lives without continually thinking about the old place."

"Thanks. Anyway, I thought I'd show him the beautiful Welsh scenery."

"I'm not sure about Llaneirw being that beautiful, but if you take him to some of the beauty spots, then yes, it is. It's really the only thing I miss about living in Llaneirw. I loved being near the sea. Do you miss it?"

Kyra looked over at Fran, who stared into space. She wondered if Fran was imagining the village in her head. Kyra hesitated. "I thought I'd miss the sea. Especially as I'd lived relatively near the sea in Whittingbury, too, but I like Manchester. It has a buzz about it that neither of those two places had. And when I go to Stockholm, I'm surrounded by lots of water there. I have the best of both worlds."

"Ooh, so you're going to Stockholm again? Is it serious between you and Nils?"

"Not serious, but I like him a lot and he seems to feel the same way. We're planning to move between here and there over the next few months to see how it goes. It's lucky we both have similar jobs and can work from home if needed."

Fran walked back from taking some of the dirty plates over to the sink. Hugging Kyra, she said, "I'm glad you've found someone and especially someone who understands what you do.

Now, I'm going to bed, so I can get up at silly-o'clock in the morning for my shift. Night."

~

Kyra stood in Arrivals waiting for Nils to appear. As soon as he saw her, his face lit up into a broad smile. She was getting used to having to stretch up to kiss him. Nils hugged her, so close she could barely breathe; the kiss lingered longer and longer, until she had to break away.

"You're not supposed to kill me by kiss." Kyra laughed. "Can you see the headline? 'Woman found dead after being kissed by dangerous Swedish killer.'"

They both burst out laughing.

"But I've missed you so much," Nils responded, trying to grab her again.

"Come on, you're making a spectacle of us both. Anyway, you only saw me last week."

"I know, but the more I see you, the more I want to be with you."

Kyra thought he was joking, but Nils looked serious. Her insides quivered at the thought of him wanting to be with her.

"Let's get back to my little house, and I can introduce you..."

"To the bedroom?"

Kyra hit him. "Man, you have one thing on your mind." Grabbing his hand, she led him out of the airport to the car park.

Kyra smiled to herself, glad Fran hadn't got home yet, because the scenario was very similar to her first arrival at Nils' flat in Stockholm. As soon as they got through the door, Nils began undressing her, demanding to be introduced to the bedroom.

Giggling, they fell on the bed, where they remained for the rest of the afternoon.

Later, Kyra presented Nils with one of her mum's recipes: jerk chicken with rice and plantain. She'd cooked for him while they were in Sweden, but now they were in her home, she enjoyed cooking him something that belonged to part of her cultural background. While they were drinking coffee, Kyra received a text from Fran to say they were short-handed, so she was staying over at the hospital for the next few days.

Two days later, Kyra drove Nils over to Llaneirw. Probably due to his size, Nils was a fidgety passenger. He didn't seem able to get the car seat far enough back to stretch his legs out fully. However, he soon forgot his discomfort, fascinated by some of the place names he saw on road signs. One in particular made him smile. Hearing him trying to pronounce *Bodelwyddan*, Kyra couldn't help but laugh, especially as she had an equally difficult time pronouncing many Welsh words.

Their drive skirted around the edge of Chester, the largest town since leaving Manchester, and they took the A55, the North Wales Expressway. The next largest place they passed was St Asaph, which Kyra also didn't know how to pronounce. Nils showed his surprise at how few trees there were as they drove through the Welsh countryside.

"We've got so many trees in Sweden. It's odd seeing so few. I'd forgotten how few trees there were here, and how many we have at home. Did you know that seventy percent of Sweden is covered in forest?"

"Wow, no, I didn't know that fact. That's pretty amazing. It also explains how easy it is for Swedish killers to bury people in the forest and their bodies remain lost for so long."

Out of the corner of her eye, she noticed Nils give her a weird look.

"I watch a lot of Scandi TV dramas, and I've always thought how handy the forests are for getting rid of dead bodies."

Nils laughed.

Kyra continued. "A handy place, if you get fed up with girlfriends or wives."

"Mm, and you'd better remember that, Miss Jackson!"

On reaching Abergele, they could finally see the coast. Even though they'd been able to glimpse the coastline from several points, this was the first time they were actually next to the sea and eventually had a great view of Colwyn Bay. Then as they left Colwyn, the road took them away from the sea where, at Llandudno Junction, they drove under the River Conwy. They remained alongside the coast until they pulled off the Expressway into Llaneirw about an hour and a half after they had left Manchester.

Kyra had warned Nils several times that it wasn't a place of outstanding beauty, but as she drove into Llaneirw village and parked up at the Blue Dolphin, he said, "It has character. It's very quaint." He got out of the car and immediately started stretching.

"My car isn't that small!"

"It is for my legs. I rarely travel in cars these days, because at home I walk everywhere, or get the metro or train."

"Come on, we'll get something to eat, and then we'll go over to the estate agent and see how things are going."

Kyra led him into the pub, and after ordering drinks, they sat perusing the menu.

"What's a good choice?" Nils asked.

"Most things, to be honest, but they do a great fish and chips, with the fish in beer batter."

"Okay, I'll go with that."

They settled down to their lunch.

After lunch, Kyra arranged to leave her car parked in the pub car park, while they went into town to talk to the estate agent. Kyra gave Nils a quick guided tour of the beachfront at Llaneirw. First she showed him where Jess had lived with her dad, then the café where Danny's girlfriend had lived, before leading him through the underpass into the new town.

Kyra felt her stomach tightly knot as she and Nils entered the house where she'd lived with her mum and sister, but if she wanted their relationship to work, she knew she had to be more open. As they walked around the house, even though she hadn't lived there all her life as Fran had, tears began to fill her eyes. Nils put his arm around her.

"Are you okay?"

Kyra blew her nose and wiped her eyes. "Yes, sorry. I was being nostalgic for something that never happened."

He gave her an odd look.

"I didn't spend my childhood here. I lived with my dad in Bideford until he died. I only moved here to help Fran, because Mum's mental health was deteriorating."

"So, you grew up together – you and Fran?"

"No. Mum left my dad when I was six. She moved here and then gave birth to Fran."

Nils raised his eyebrows. Before he could say anything, Kyra continued. "She is my dad's, but Mum had just had enough of the comments when people saw her with me. I'm so much paler than my mum, and they often didn't realise I was her daughter. It's odd really, because Fran is slightly paler skinned than me, and it didn't bother Mum in Wales. I think, because some of her family lived nearby, so she had more support. Anyway, Dad brought me up, and I had a great time, plus he gave me a lot of leeway as a teenager – he taught me to be independent."

Nils laughed. "Sometimes a little too independent."

"Hey, you wouldn't want a clingy girlfriend, would you?"

"True." He bent down and kissed her.

“Anyway, as I told you, Mum died. She killed herself. Took an overdose of her pills.”

It seemed Nils didn’t know what to say. They remained quiet for a while, hugging each other.

Kyra spoke first. “And here we are today, about to sell this house once and for all. Come on, we’ll get a coffee and I can leave you in the café while I go to see the estate agent. I shouldn’t be too long.”

The walk from the house into the centre of modern Llaneirw wasn’t too long, and Nils was soon ensconced with coffee, a Welsh cake and muffin while Kyra went off to her meeting.

Later, after an hour and a half drive back to Manchester, they got some snacks and spent the evening cuddled up under a blanket in the garden, drinking wine, listening to music and star gazing. Comfortable in each other’s company.

10

Next morning, Nil wandered into the kitchen to make himself and Kyra a wake-up coffee. He had a shock when, half way through the preparation, Fran walked in, coming face-to-face with him – a very tall, naked man.

Completely nonplussed, she looked him up and down, and said, “Hi, Nils, good to meet you. Kyra said you were fit.” She walked past him and continued to get her own breakfast.

Nils, who wasn’t usually embarrassed, on this occasion, felt himself turning red. As soon as the coffee was ready, he made a quick exit.

Having heard the whole encounter, Kyra had to abruptly sit up in bed because she’d laughed so much she made herself cough.

“Well, you are fit. There’s no denying that, but I didn’t expect my sister to see the whole package all in one go.”

Nils put the coffee safely on the dressing table and threw a cushion at Kyra.

“I was going to introduce you later, over lunch.”

Nils passed Kyra her coffee. “Well, I think we’ve got to know each other quite well.”

When they eventually surfaced for their breakfast, Fran had already disappeared to the shops. Kyra had left a list of groceries they needed for their meal, and Fran had obviously decided to take control and go shopping. Nils and Kyra were clearing away their breakfast dishes when she returned.

"I don't think I need to introduce you to Nils, as you've already met," Kyra said, embarrassing him again.

Fran smiled and continued to unpack the bags of food. Nils was relieved the atmosphere was soon relaxed and happy as they chatted away while Kyra and Fran prepared their late lunch. Nils listened with interest as Fran answered his questions about her nursing course, and Kyra watched them both, looking contented that they were hitting it off so well.

The rest of the week, Kyra introduced Nils to the joys of Didsbury. She took him to several of her favourite local eateries rather than cook each night. Nils knew she actually enjoyed cooking, but she also enjoyed eating out. *Salmon's Leap* was her go-to when it came to a fish restaurant, she told him, explaining that she knew how much fish and seafood Swedes ate, so she wanted to show him he could get good food in Manchester too.

"Oh, *Sal-mon's Leap*. This is your favourite?" Nils said, sounding the '*l*'.

Kyra smiled to herself.

"What are you smiling about?" Nils asked.

"I'm sorry, I'm not laughing, but it just made me smile, because we don't pronounce the '*l*' in salmon. It's silent. English is an odd language, at times."

"So, no '*l*'? My teacher taught us all wrong then. She taught us to say it that way."

"But it's not surprising. I don't know why we don't say the '*l*', either. We just don't."

"I'll try and remember."

"Don't, it's cute."

“Cute! You think I’m cute. All one hundred and ninety-four centimetres of me?” Nils laughed.

“You’re not cute, but the way you say sal-mon is,” Kyra said, between giggles.

Despite the pronunciation issue, the night went well and Nils came away having made the decision that Sal-mon’s Leap was his favourite restaurant too.

A few days later, they were preparing to drive to the University of Manchester for Kyra’s lecture at the journalists’ conference. When her university professor had suggested her to the organisers, she had been both surprised and grateful, as it would be a good opportunity to meet other people in her sector and show off her presentation skills. Nils had mentioned how much he also looked forward to hearing her speak – though Kyra knew she would feel a little nervous about talking in front of him.

Walking from where they had parked the car, Kyra chatted away with animated energy, and she knew she was feeling a mixture of excitement and pre-performance nerves. Although they arrived at the building in good time so Kyra could set up her presentation, the doorman barred their entrance.

“Excuse me, but I’m supposed to be in the Jacobson Suite,” Kyra said.

“Kitchen staff are around the back, not this entrance,” the burly guard commanded.

“I’m sorry? I’m the speaker here tonight,” Kyra replied.

The guard stared at her. “Oh, I thought you were kitchen staff arriving late.”

“And why would you think that?” Kyra asked, although she already knew.

"Erm...you didn't look like you were the speaker."

"What should a speaker look like?" she asked in the most innocent tone she could muster.

The guard blustered and looked embarrassed, unable to give her an answer. He opened the door and stood aside so Kyra and Nils could enter.

Nils looked as though he were about to deck the guard, so Kyra pulled him through the door after her.

"Are you just going to accept that?" he asked.

"Yes. What would you like me to do, lose my control and yell at him?"

"Well, I can certainly tell him what I think."

"Nils, just leave it. I'm here, and the man is an ignorant idiot. He's not worth me wasting my breath on him. Plus, I don't want to get blood on my outfit," she added flippantly, hoping to defuse the situation.

Nils' jaw tensed and she could see that he was still up for confronting the guard.

"Nils, I'm old enough to take care of myself, and it's nothing new. Things have got better, but there are still very stupid people out there, and I'm not giving credence to their beliefs or ideas by rising to them."

"But I don't want someone treating you like that."

"Nils, you can't change some people's behaviour by shouting. Then you're no better than him. Besides, I don't need a man to fight my battles for me. Okay?"

Kyra marched ahead, leaving Nils trying to control himself.

Once they arrived in the conference hall, the professor who had invited her to talk greeted them both. Nils took the bag he was carrying over to the podium and then sat down out of the way.

Completely unfazed, Kyra went on to deliver a brilliant talk, and she referred to Nils on several occasions. There were lots of questions, which she answered confidently.

Luckily, by the time they left, the burly guard had already gone, which meant no opportunity for Nils to vent his anger at him.

On the way home, Kyra could tell Nils was still sulking about her not-needing-a-man comment. Fran had just arrived home, too, and asked how everything went. Kyra answered, "Fine," but Nils answered, "Okay, apart from an ignorant guard."

Kyra just smiled at Fran. "The usual old prejudice about my capabilities."

"Oh, that!" Fran answered.

Nils clearly couldn't cope with their blasé acceptance.

"Are people often so obviously prejudiced?" he asked.

"Not everyone is, but when you do meet the idiots, then yes, they are." Fran answered for them both.

"Nils wanted to beat him up, Fran."

"No, I just wanted to protect you from him."

"I told you, I don't need protecting."

"But I care about you, so of course I want to help."

Kyra expected Fran could hear his frustration and the building awkwardness; she slipped out and went upstairs.

"I know you care, and that's great, but if we're together, then you have to accept that I can stand up for myself. Okay? I'll report him to the university."

Nils was about to open his mouth, but Kyra continued.

"It's not a problem you will ever have. You're a man, for one, and two, more importantly, you're white, so it will never happen to you."

"So, am I supposed to stand by and see you insulted?" Nils asked.

"Just let me deal with it in my own way. If I didn't, then I'd never cope. Knowing that you care is the most important thing to me, but let me live my life as I choose. And…" She kissed him. "I choose to be with…" She kissed him again. "You." This time, Kyra pulled him down towards her and kissed him passionately.

Nils responded by picking her up and carrying her upstairs. "Okay," he managed to say between their kisses.

11

EARLY JULY, 2023
MANCHESTER

Lukas slammed the front door of their apartment and rushed into the lounge, where Jess was finishing off a report she needed to hand in by the beginning of the next week.

She looked up at him with an expression of annoyance. "What—?"

"I can't believe it. Cole has resigned. He contacted the office while we were away. He didn't even talk to me about it first. I don't know what he's thinking. He could easily have continued in a different role. He could've worked in the office in the UK – he wouldn't have to travel again. I don't understand it." Lukas took a breath as he grabbed a beer from the fridge.

"Maybe the accident made him rethink how he's living his life," Jess said tentatively.

Lukas grimaced. "I thought he was living the life he wanted to live – predominantly helping other people. That's why he was so passionate about joining the company in the first place. I don't get it."

"I supposed this is a complete one-eighty turn in his thinking. He must have a good reason. Surely?"

Lukas took several long sips of his beer. "I don't know. There's something different about him." He paused. "Don't laugh, but when he used to look at me, there was a connection in his eyes. I don't see it anymore." Looking at Jess, he asked, "Does that make me sound mad?"

"No madder than me seeing ghosts!" she laughed.

Lukas gave her a *don't-go-there* look.

"Seriously," she continued, "he must be feeling very different after being involved in a life-threatening accident. If you think there are other differences, why don't you talk to Sofia? She might be feeling the same."

"I think I might. It'll be interesting to see if she's noticed anything too."

Jess leant in and kissed him. "You wait, in a few months, he'll be back to normal. Come on, you chill and I'll sort dinner."

Lukas laughed as they moved into the beautiful modern kitchen that stood at one end of the lounge. He knew this was one of the reasons why Jess loved the apartment so much. When they had guests, even though he usually did the main cooking, Jess could help out and still carry on a conversation with anyone else in the room. They always joked that she was his *sous-chef*. The size of the apartment meant there was even enough room for a dining table between the kitchen and lounge. When they'd viewed the apartment, Jess had explained this had been the idea her dad had been aiming for in their house in Llaneirw, the main difference being that this apartment had top of the range fittings and equipment, which the house in Llaneirw hadn't had.

"So, how am I going to chill when you're doing the cooking?"

"Don't be cheeky, I've got it planned."

Luckily, Jess had bought two M&S ready-meals earlier in the day. They wouldn't take long to prepare, which Lukas was grateful for. Hot food and a few glasses of wine would soon calm him down.

A few days later, after checking she would be at home, Lukas dropped round to see how Sofia was getting on. She seemed pleased to see him, and she told him how well Cole had recovered and that he'd actually been home for the last few weeks – in fact, since they'd been away for Midsummer. He'd just gone to the hospital for some extra tests, to check that his leg had healed as they'd expected after the operation. Hopefully they'd remove his bandages, too, she'd said.

"He'll be sorry he missed you, Lukas."

Lukas wasn't sure he believed that. Over a coffee, after answering Sofia's questions about the Midsummer celebrations in Sweden, Lukas tried to drop the odd question into the conversation about how Cole appeared to her. Her answers were evasive. She told Lukas that Cole was reticent to talk about the accident, but she understood why, because it must have been pretty traumatic. Though now he'd come back home, she'd noticed him beginning to relax and become more himself. Typically, rather than accept the changes that Cole's injuries must have made to him mentally, Sofia's interest lay in talking about what they would do when he was back to complete fitness.

Not fully concentrating on what she was saying, Lukas recalled the only thing that Cole ever complained about: that Sofia always wanted more. She liked the latest gadget in the apartment, the latest fashion. Money never bothered her, and Lukas always reminded Cole that was precisely because it wasn't hers! But Cole seemed blind when it came to Sofia. He just wanted to make her happy, and if that meant spending money, that's what it took.

Lukas became aware that Sofia had asked him a question.

"I'm sorry, I just remembered something Cole used to say. I didn't catch what you said."

Sofia repeated what she'd asked. "We're thinking about going on holiday in a few weeks. What do you think?"

"Holiday? Have you asked the doctors if he's fit enough? Does he want to go on holiday after what he's been through?"

"Yeah, we talked about it. He's far more relaxed now he's out of hospital. I mean, it wasn't very nice in there and some warm weather would do him the world of good. We wouldn't go for long, but I think it would be perfect for us both."

"Mm." Lukas couldn't think of anything else to say about the matter. "I presume he has told you that he's resigned?"

"Yes, he has."

"Sofia, has Cole told you anything about the accident, or before it? I mean, do you know if he was in any trouble?"

Sofia looked surprised. "What sort of trouble? No. As you know, he can't remember anything about the accident, but he hasn't mentioned any problems out there. And he didn't when I had a call with him when he first arrived in Ethiopia. He was very upbeat about it all."

"But he's suddenly decided to resign. Don't you think that's odd?"

"Not really. He nearly died. That's a life-changing event, so he's decided to make some changes to his life. I don't think it's so shocking. Anyway, once the insurance money comes through, we'll be okay financially, so he's not worried about giving up this job." Sofia smiled.

Lukas hadn't considered the fact that Cole would claim on insurance. And again, it didn't seem like the first thing his friend would be concentrating on. It certainly wasn't what the Cole he knew would do.

"What insurance is he claiming on?" Lukas asked, although he had a suspicion that he probably already knew.

Sofia looked a little awkward, which was a first for her. Usually nothing seemed to faze her. "Er, I think he's asked his solicitor to look into the company that were driving him on the day of the accident."

Lukas was taken aback. Ethiopia wasn't a rich country, which was why Andersson Global were working there to supply pumps to provide fresh water systems. For Cole to go after that company seemed very disingenuous, no matter what accident he'd had. And, yes, Cole had been badly injured, but Andersson's had made sure he got the best medical attention possible. In fact, the more he thought about it, the more he realised that it was probably Andersson Global's insurance that would be paying out, as they'd been responsible for arranging the outing he'd been on.

Sofia's bit of news put Lukas in an even more unsettled mood about the version of Cole that had returned from Africa. Making excuses, he left not long afterwards.

~

For the second time that week, on returning home, Lukas slammed the door as he entered the apartment. "Jess! It's worse than I thought."

Jess, who was chatting to her dad on FaceTime, signalled for Lukas to keep quiet.

"Dad, it's Lukas, he's just got in."

"Hi, Lukas," Danny shouted.

Lukas walked over to look at the screen and waved back. "Hi, Danny. Hope you're both okay?"

"Yes, we're great, thanks. Sorry to hear about your friend. I hope he's fully recovered soon."

"Thanks, Danny. Me too. See you again." Lukas kissed Jess and wandered over to the lounge to pour himself a strong drink.

He heard Jess end the call early, telling her dad she'd catch up with him another time.

"Can you pour me one too?" she said.

Lukas poured another drink.

"So, what's happened that got you so mad this time?" Jess asked.

"I don't know where to start." He slumped down onto the sofa. "Well, not only has Cole resigned, but he's also claiming against the insurance." He took a large swig of his drink. "As if we weren't going to look after him. I mean, if it wasn't for Dad, he'd probably not be here in one piece. How ungrateful is that?"

Out of the corner of his eye, he noticed Jess about to answer, but as it was a rhetorical question, he continued ranting. "Worse still, he is going to sue the company that was driving him. Cole would never have done that. This just isn't right." Lukas ran his hand through his hair, making it stand on end.

"What can I do?" Jess asked.

"Nothing. I'm sorry but I just needed a rant. Come here."

She moved next to him, put her drink on the coffee table, and put her arms around him. Lukas buried his head in her shoulder. She held him tight. At that moment, he felt her being motherly, rather than being his amorous girlfriend.

"This will all sort itself out, I'm sure. You just need to give him time."

From his slumped posture, Lukas pulled himself up straight, downed his whisky and said, "God, I'm so glad you're here, Jess Graham!" Then he kissed her in a way he would never kiss his mother.

12

Sofia mulled over the conversation she'd had with Lukas. She had to agree with him: Cole was different. But as she'd told him, after what Cole had been through, it didn't seem surprising.

Cole looked comfortable, relaxing with his cup of coffee. Since he'd come home a month ago, she'd been pussy-footing around him. Too scared to be overly demonstrative, she'd not wanted to hug him too hard or kiss him too passionately, worried she might break him. Her choice of sleeping arrangements hadn't pleased Cole initially, though when she thought about it, he hadn't put up a huge argument against it, either.

She noticed how fit he looked, apart from his left leg, which occasionally caused him a little pain when he walked. In fact, he looked more toned than she'd ever seen him look before, which was odd, considering what he'd been through during the last weeks. Maybe she'd imagined it. And she'd also noticed him doing a thing with his good leg – tapping his foot on the floor so that his leg shook, which she'd never seen him do before. She did vaguely remember his brother doing that. *Very odd – perhaps it's the stress of the accident?*

"Do you want another coffee, babes?" she asked, walking over to the kitchen area.

"Yeah, but I'll get it. The doctor said I've got to use my leg as much as possible."

Although he'd been given the 'all clear' from the hospital and had been told it was up to him to carefully build up his strength, he occasionally felt some pain and continued to limp slightly, as he did now, walking over to kiss her. As if he'd been invading her earlier thoughts, he asked, "Don't you think it's time we slept in the same bed? I think I'm more or less bruiseless, if there's such a word." He laughed. "I don't think you'll hurt me." He kissed her again.

There was something different about his kiss, but Sofia couldn't work out what. He even smelt different. *Wow, I must be imagining things. Do I really remember what he smelt like? Maybe it's the hospital smell still on him,* she wondered, although she couldn't see how. She was annoyed with herself, because this was certainly her husband standing in front of her. She couldn't deny that. But there was definitely a change about him that she could not describe.

Looking into his beautiful green eyes, she stretched over to return the kiss. The kiss lingered and Cole pulled her towards him, running his hands down her back and over her bum. Feeling a surge of excitement through her body, she leant in closer, and in doing so, managed to knock his bad leg against the kitchen island. Cole winced. Instantly, she pulled away from him. "God, I'm sorry, babe. I didn't mean to hurt you."

"Don't be silly, you can never hurt me." He smacked her bottom. "Do you fancy looking through some of our photos? They might help bring some of my memory back."

"That's a great idea. I'll grab my laptop." Although her mobile held loads of selfies she'd taken for her Insta feed, she'd uploaded their holiday snaps and many of the others they'd taken over the years to her laptop. Sitting on the sofa, they looked through the images, with Sofia giving a running commentary. Occasionally, she'd ask, "Do you remember that?" Or comment, "He was so funny, wasn't he? That was such a good holiday."

Cole nodded but kept fairly quiet, trying to concentrate on who the people were that Sofia referred to as friends. He didn't know any of them. How could he have ever managed his job if he couldn't even remember who people were?

"Did that help?" Sofia said, looking at Cole. He hadn't seemed to remember very many people at all. Maybe he was still tired. She decided the pain in his leg must have robbed him of his energy. "You'll soon be fine when we start seeing people. Especially when you see Lukas and Jess. He was sorry he missed you yesterday when he popped round. We'll make a date to catch up with them soon."

Cole gave her a smile, although a little feeble. "Hopefully."

"Come on, let's have something to eat. That'll make you feel better."

Sofia went over to the kitchen and set about heating up one of the many meals she had in the freezer. Cooking wasn't a skill either of them had. Not that it mattered, because prior to Cole's accident, they'd rarely eaten at home.

After their meal, they settled down to watch some TV together until Cole said, "I'm ready for bed. Are you going to join me tonight?" He held out his hand. Sofia pulled herself up, took his hand, and followed him into their bedroom.

As Cole began to undress, Sofia realised she hadn't actually seen him naked since he'd come home from the hospital. He'd always kept to himself when he showered or got ready for bed. Now, as he removed his shirt, she took a quick intake of breath. He definitely looked more muscular than she'd remembered.

Cole must have heard her. Sitting down on the edge of the

bed, he beckoned to her. "Help me undress. I'm not good at keeping my balance when I'm tired."

"That's a good one." Laughing, she knelt on the floor in front of him and stretched up to kiss his lips before starting to remove his jeans. She was interrupted as Cole ran his hands inside her top and began fondling her breasts. Unable to continue, she quickly pulled off her top and leant forward, kissing his chest while he undid her bra. Cole pushed himself further up the bed, and as he did so, Sofia finally managed to remove his jeans. She crawled up the bed after him and they began kissing passionately, their hands caressing each other's bodies. At one point, Sofia caught sight of a small tattoo on Cole's hip, which hadn't been there when he went away.

Cole removed the last of their clothes and began to explore Sofia's body with his hands and his mouth. An even more noticeable difference: he had far more confidence in his lovemaking than he'd ever had prior to his accident. Again, she put it down to his brush with death. Whatever this change was, she didn't care. Any worries she had were completely erased; she was in heaven.

Her whole body tingled with excitement and expectation as his attention moved between her legs. When he eventually entered her, in the midst of her ecstasy, she cried out his name.

"Caleb."

13

Entwined, in a knot of arms and legs, Caleb and Sofia lay side by side, both breathing heavily.

When his breath slowed, Caleb asked, "When did you know for certain it was me?"

Sofia didn't respond for a while.

"I've been noticing you were different, but when we were in bed, I wondered why you had suddenly become such a good lover. I thought probably because you nearly died, you know, the whole, '*wanting to make the most of life*'." She paused, caressing his face before continuing. "When you did that thing with your tongue – Cole never did that – you're the only person I've slept with that did. It brought all my feelings back from when we were younger, you know? But it confused me – you're dead, so how could it be you? I still wasn't sure, but then the passion I felt the more we made love, and when you moved inside me"—she shut her eyes, inhaled, and ran her tongue over her lips—"then I knew for certain."

Caleb leant over and gave Sofia another lingering and passionate kiss. "Just for you to double check you're right." He smiled at her. "Didn't you notice any other things?"

Sofia moved away from him and sat up in the bed. "Well, then there were all the times you didn't recognise people, even Lukas. Initially, I put it down to your head injury, but I noticed that when we met other people, I always had to remind you who they were. I tried not to make it too obvious. And, there were other small things too—"

"Like?" Caleb interrupted.

"Well, when you were younger, how you smiled at me – when you knew I fancied you. You always had a little crooked smile and I'd started noticing that when you smiled at me. But just thought I was imagining it. And, just when did you get that tattoo on your hip?"

Ignoring the last question, he said, "You know you're brilliant. You've saved me so many times over the last few weeks. I could have completely blown it, because apart from you, I didn't know anyone."

Caleb kissed her again, and Sofia responded with an equal passion.

She pulled away and said, "Would your nan recognise which twin you are? Is that why you don't want to see her?"

"Yeah. She could always tell the difference between us. In fact, the only person, so I can't chance her knowing the truth."

He could tell Sofia hadn't considered the reality of it all. He waited for it to sink in and for her to ask the main question. Although a little scared of her response, he prompted her. "Don't you want to know why I'm pretending to be Cole?"

Sofia stayed quiet for longer than he liked. He took her hand and looked into her eyes. "Do you want to know?" he asked.

"To be honest, yes and no. God, when we made love, it was mind-blowing. I mean, Cole hasn't made me feel like that for ages." She paused. "Honestly, ever!"

Caleb started to say something, but Sofia continued, her eyes all the while fixed on his hand, which held her own.

"I didn't know for sure you weren't Cole, though when we made love, that clinched it. But, I had been wondering why there were so many things that seemed different. The main one: Cole loved his job and he'd never have resigned. I think he loved it more than me, to be honest. But, don't get me wrong, he was always kind and bought me everything I ever wanted. Selfishly, I worried when I heard he'd been in an accident, and hoped it wouldn't be anything life-threatening. I couldn't have coped if he'd come back without an arm or leg, you know. But even though you were hurt bad, I'm glad you've recovered." She took a deep breath. "So, do I want to know why you're here and he's not? No, not if you hurt him in any way. Not if they're going to take you away from me again."

He held her face in both his hands and looked directly into her eyes. "I promise I didn't hurt him."

Sofia looked relieved, but for the first time, fierce too. Moving away from him, after a long pause, she said, "You know, I grieved for years over your death. Even when Cole and I were first married, whenever I looked at him, I could see you, and it always hurt. Deep down in my heart, I had wanted to be your wife, not his. When you went to prison, although I didn't know the whole story, I was so angry that you'd got caught up in that...that shit, but then when they said you'd killed yourself, I almost lost it. You know, Cole and me got together because he looked after me through all that time?" She didn't wait for an answer. "Though when we heard you were dead, to start with, Cole couldn't console me for weeks, but he kept coming back to me. He always cared. Not once did he complain about how I must have made him feel – second choice. Not once!"

For the first time as she looked up at his face, her eyes were full of tears. Though he was a little uncertain who they were for, he understood he was safe. She wanted him, Caleb, not Cole.

Her voice quavering, she asked, "How could you do that to

me? Why didn't you come back to me when you came out of prison?"

"Sofe, I'm sorry. I couldn't. They'd have threatened you and Cole and Nan. I couldn't chance it."

"Who? Who would have threatened us?"

Caleb stopped any further questions by pulling her back towards him and kissing her.

"God, I should have made you my girl once and for all when we were teenagers and not messed around. Then I might not have got caught up in that stuff." Caleb kissed her again. "Oh, and by the way, that's when I got the tattoo. When we were still at school. Sometime after we weren't seeing each other as much. I got it to keep you close to me."

He kissed her again, and soon, it appeared he'd made her forget her question. They lay in bed holding on to each other, letting go of their pent up passion, making up for all the lost years.

Finally, Caleb made a move. He managed to get up, though rather stiffly after the exertions he'd gladly put his body through. Now he had to tell her everything. He put on a jumper and his joggers and walked into the kitchen.

"I'll make us a coffee, and then I'll explain."

He left Sofia putting on the cuddly onesie she liked to lounge around in, then she followed him.

They sat on the sofa. Caleb leant forward, his elbows on his knees, gazing straight ahead, while Sofia sat at the other end, with her knees tucked up under her, cradling a large mug of coffee.

After a short time, Caleb rubbed his hand around the back of his neck then stretched before turning to face Sofia.

"I don't know where to start, but I'll tell you what happened from the beginning. Okay?"

"Yeah, however bad – I want to hear it all."

14

Caleb took his time to speak. "I don't know where to begin, but I suppose how I ended up in prison?"

"That would be a good start. I never understood how you got caught up in all of that stuff."

"Do you remember that time when I got picked up at that club, *Linkers*?"

Sofia nodded.

"Well, loads of us got carted off to the nick, and I met this kid called Jaz. We just hit it off straight away. He had something about him." He paused. "Anyway, he said his dad would get us out, and true to his word, he did. This older guy turned up, and before we knew it, we were both out and in the back of his swanky car. His dad seemed to have some clout with the police. But it was actually way more than that. It turned out I'd only made friends with Jaz Johnson, whose dad, Tony Johnson, ran one of the biggest gangs in Liverpool at that time. He had connections. Though I didn't realise how big they were. It seems they were linked to an organised crime gang based in Amsterdam. You must have read some of that in the newspapers?"

"Yes, some, but I didn't take it all in, and I hated reading about you. I didn't want to hear anything about it, to be honest. My dad went ballistic when he knew that you'd been arrested. Told me never to see you again."

"I'm not surprised about your dad. Not that he had anything to be smug about – sorry, that was mean."

"No, it's the truth. It wasn't like he was squeaky clean. Anyway, how did you get involved in it all? I mean, we weren't seeing each other as much, then. Whenever I wanted to see you, you'd make some excuse."

"That's because, over time, I became more and more involved in the business of the gang, and I didn't want to get you mixed up in it too. To start with, just small things, making deliveries of drugs, money, collecting money – small stuff. Then they organised a big drugs heist.

"The night arrived, and following the Transit in which most of the men were travelling, I drove Jaz, Tony and the closest members of his crew to the destination I'd been given. When we arrived, Tony suddenly seemed annoyed that Jaz had come along. He told him to swap places with me, and told me to go in with the guys, and just carry stuff out to the Transit when told to. Jaz seemed happy not to be taking part, but unhappy that I was going in his place.

"I just thought I'd do whatever they directed me to do. I mean, how difficult could it be? We'd grab the stuff, and then off we'd go."

Caleb took a drink of his now lukewarm coffee.

"How stupid could I have been? From the beginning it all went so wrong. The security guard that should have been on duty had phoned in sick, so the guy we came across wasn't expecting us. He drew his weapon, which I'm sure he'd never actually used. One of our guys, Jackson, shot him before the poor guy could even think of returning fire. I felt sick and stood glued to the spot. I hadn't bargained for any shooting. One of the older men shoved a large bag in my arms, saying, ‘Grow a pair, lad, stop gawping, and get a move on. Put it in the Transit.’ I didn’t even consider arguing.

“I ran backward and forward as we filled the Transit and the getaway car with the drugs. We’d nearly filled the van when we heard the sirens. Tony and his closest team ran for the car where Jaz sat with the engine idling. He yelled at me to get a move on, but one of the older men threw another bag at me to put in the Transit. Jaz drove off, and by the time the police arrived, some of the crew had run, and along with a few others, I was caught. In the scrummage as people were trying to escape, the guy who’d shot the guard managed to get away too.

“I’d never felt as terrified as I did when we got to the police station, because of the seriousness of what had happened. Someone had been killed. I hadn’t done it, but even I knew that I’d be in deep shit for just having been there. The next day, after being questioned, the news that I’d be lucky if I’d be free before my thirtieth birthday panicked me. I tried to protest my innocence, saying I’d never been in trouble with the police before and I hadn’t been involved in the shooting, but of course, all in vain.

“I didn’t see any of the other guys who were picked up, so I didn’t know who they’d caught and who’d got free.

“One of the guys questioning me asked if I knew the name of the gang boss. I kept quiet. I didn’t want to be a snitch. But they kept on at me, and when they offered me a chance of my jail time being cut, I considered their questions. But I had another moment of panic when I realised that if I turned evidence against Tony, he’d come after me. After much deliberation and trying to get me to give them names, my solicitor told me that if I helped them with the names of the main man, they’d ask for me to be placed away from any members of the OCG. They gave me assurances that they’d do everything in their power to make sure I was kept safe.”

"What's the OCG?" Sofia asked.

"Police jargon for Organised Crime Gang." Caleb carried on. "Of course, what I didn't know then was that they could only ask for that consideration, but basically the decision would be made by prison service as to where I'd serve my time.

"Again, my solicitor talked to me, telling me my best option would be to take the offer. I could get as little as seven years, and even be out after three, if I told the police what they wanted to know. I slept on it.

"The next morning, I gave Tony up, and they showed me photos, asking if I recognised any of the other men. I recognised them all, as they were all the other members of his gang, including Jackson, who'd killed the guard. I also told them the name of Tony's contact in Amsterdam. The head of the OCG – Marius de Haan. I'd overheard Tony talking about him and remembered the name, because it sounded unusual. More than anything, they were most interested in him and the link between the Johnsons and de Haan.

"And then it dawned on me that I might have done the wrong thing. Tiredness had probably made me say more than I should have done. I felt sick when I was back in my cell and I thought about what might happen to me if either the Johnsons or de Haan found out it was me who'd turned them in."

"Did Jaz get caught too?" Sofia asked.

"No. I heard later from Jaz that his dad had been picked up from the club, where they'd found him playing cards with some of the other guys. They were so confident that nobody would bother them. They also took Jaz in for questioning, but there wasn't any forensic evidence that proved he'd ever been present at the heist.

"They'd got evidence about the shooting, because I'd pointed out the guy in the photo, plus when they picked him up the daft idiot still had the gun on him! Although, the gang burnt the car – again, something Jaz told me later – and the police did find some of the drugs at Tony's house, so they nicked him.

"Luckily, because the prison service took into consideration that I hadn't previously offended and the prison I ended up in had no links with the other members of the OCG, it meant Jaz could visit me. I had to give my permission for him to visit, because of his link to the gang. However, he wanted out of the lifestyle his dad had built. Nan and Cole had turned their backs on me, wanting nothing to do with me, plus none of us knew Mum's whereabouts, so I was particularly grateful for Jaz's visits."

"So, how come you 'died'?"

"Well, Jaz told me that Tony had spread the threat, and that if I didn't leave the UK, then when I left prison, I'd be a dead man. Astonishingly, he promised to leave my family alone, as he knew they had nothing to do with me, anyway. This is when Jaz suggested the idea of killing me off. It would mean I didn't have to keep looking over my shoulder.

"We then hatched a plan that when I left prison, we'd 'kill me off', so that my family didn't bother me, and also his dad wouldn't need to look for me."

"But, surely, it was ages ago. Won't they have got on with their lives?"

Caleb took a deep breath, trying to calm himself. "Don't be so naïve, Sofe. Of course they want me dead. Thanks to me, the whole gang got banged up, and Tony died in prison. Of course they want revenge. If the gang knew I'd set foot in the UK, and if they find out I'm here now, I really will be a dead man."

Sofia looked contrite. He knew she hadn't meant to annoy him, but he could tell that his reaction had scared her. Noticing, he leant over and kissed her.

She asked another question. "I sort of understand, but why

couldn't you get a message to me so that I knew you weren't really dead?"

Caleb let out a long sigh. "Haven't you been listening? The Johnson gang would have known. Your demeanour would have been totally different if you'd thought I was alive."

"What, you mean they'd have been watching me?"

"Of course. All of you. Nan, you and Cole!"

Sofia sat quietly taking all of this information in, and Caleb, seeing that she had a query, waited for her to ask her question.

"Why on earth did Jaz help you? Your evidence put his dad away."

"He helped me because he'd never really enjoyed being involved in that life. He wanted out. I already told you, it should have been me driving the getaway car, but Tony wouldn't let Jaz be involved in the actual break-in, so made him the getaway driver. As I already said, Jaz was angry with his dad about that."

"So, he helped you? How did he manage that? Surely the rest of the family were watching him?"

"Not so much. They were all rushing around, trying to sort things, especially after Tony died. I was locked up in Haverigg, far enough away from Liverpool that Jaz could visit fairly safely. If it hadn't been for him, I don't think I'd have coped doing my time, and I certainly wouldn't have got out of the country so easily."

"He's some friend."

"Yes, he is."

"Is he safe from the rest of the family now? I mean, will they ever find out that he helped you?"

Caleb shook his head. "I hope to God not."

He stood up abruptly.

"I need a stronger drink than coffee. Besides, this has gone cold. Do you want something?" he asked, going over to their small bar.

"Yes, I think I might, if you're going to tell me the rest of the story."

Caleb poured himself a whisky, and a gin and tonic for Sofia. Once he'd sat and had taken a large swig of his drink, he told her about his fake suicide, and how he'd got out of the country from Immingham as part of a container lorry crew. Then how he'd made his way across Europe, earning money doing odd jobs, working on private yachts. Occasionally delivering some suspect packages, which he thought were usually money or drugs, and then how he'd ended up in Africa.

"You have to keep this pretence going, Sofe. If any of the surviving Johnson gang find out I'm alive, both of us are in danger. I'm sorry, but Cole's death gave me an opportunity and I took it."

"I'm beginning to understand that, but what I don't understand is how you met up with Cole in Africa. What were you doing there?"

15

JULY 2023

MANCHESTER

Lukas and Jess were pleased to see Kyra and Nils when they arrived at their apartment, and they looked forward to catching up with them both again. Despite there being nearly ten years between their ages, they'd got on very well during the Midsummer festivities. When she opened the door, Jess stretched up, flung her arms around Nils' neck, gave him a big hug and kissed his cheek, and then hugged Kyra. Lukas followed suit, although he and Nils exchanged man-hugs. Lukas smiled to himself, thinking it was like one big love fest!

Lukas cooked up a concoction that he enjoyed making – prawns, salmon and pasta, with avocados and cream, plus some herbs and seasoning. The meal went down well while they reminisced about the Midsummer break, which they'd all enjoyed.

They continued to chat while Lukas cleared away the empty dishes and Jess took the dessert from the fridge. Having already drunk two bottles of wine, after their desserts, they started on a third.

Conversation after the meal turned to Nils' time in Manchester, which included grilling him on his thoughts about the city in comparison to Stockholm. Overall, he said, the city was growing on him.

"It's not quite as clean as Stockholm, but the people are incredibly friendly," he said.

"I think Kyra might have something to do with that, don't you?" Jess said.

"Erm, maybe – she is always extra friendly towards me." Nils winked.

"Why don't you guys stretch out on the comfier seats while I make the coffee?" Lukas said. He then turned to Kyra and asked, "Do you want something a bit stronger than wine to go with it? Maybe some good Swedish Aquavit?"

"Yuck, no thanks. That was the only thing I didn't fully enjoy in Sandhamn. Have you got any normal vodka or gin?"

"What, you don't like Nils' national drink?"

"Sorry but no. I don't like the taste and as hard as Nils has tried to 'educate' me, it hasn't worked. Just normal, bog-standard vodka or gin will do me fine," Kyra answered.

"You're not alone. I don't like the taste that much either," Jess said.

"It's obviously an acquired taste, for the more sophisticated palate," Nils dared to say, as Kyra jabbed him in his chest.

As they all relaxed even more, full of food, coffee and now spirits too, Lukas decided the time was right to ask his question. "I don't quite know how to broach this, but knowing that you two are invest..." He paused, the drink making his tongue feel thick. "Investigative journalists," he continued slowly, "and you've already done some great work for my dad, I wonder if you'd do some work for me?"

Nils and Kyra both looked surprised but also amused at the way Lukas had slurred.

Kyra spoke first. "It depends what it is. I hope I'm not going to be investigating more of your family?"

Lukas gave her a smile. “No, but it’s almost as bad.”

Nils stayed quiet, watching from his position – comfortably sprawled across two of the seats.

Lukas continued. “I want you to look into Cole for me.”

The silence in the room was deafening. Lukas felt awkward, but Jess gave him encouraging looks to continue.

“Ever since he’s been back from Ethiopia, he’s been different. And before you say anything about it not being surprising as he nearly died – I appreciate that. But there is something fundamentally different about him and I can’t work out what. He’s not the same man that was my best friend.”

“Have you seen Sofia and Cole recently?” Jess asked Kyra and Nils.

“Only very quickly. We bumped into them in town. Why?”

“Well, they’re behaving like they’re on their second honeymoon. They can’t leave each other alone,” Jess replied.

Lukas nodded in agreement. “It’s a bit odd. Sofia has always been very flirtatious and all over Cole, but he never responded in the same way when they were in public. Of course, I can’t say how they were *alone*, but it’s unusual for him.”

“Maybe they’re both so grateful that he’s back and fully recovered. It could have been so much worse,” Kyra said.

“I suppose. But I lived quite closely with Cole and Sofia when we were first at uni, and even then, and after they were first married...even then, they weren’t so demonstrative.”

“Showing love for each other is hardly something to make you question him,” Nils said. He then started to say something else, but changed his mind.

“How else do you think he’s different?” Kyra asked.

Lukas let out a long sigh. “I’ve been mates with Cole since we started at uni. He’s always been passionate about his work and about helping people in the world where they needed support. That’s exactly why he joined Andersson Global. But since he’s been back, he's not even asked about work. Then I found out that he's resigned, instead of taking a job somewhere else in the company, which Dad would have offered him. And, he's going to claim on the insurance. The old Cole wouldn't have done any of that."

"Do you think he's been replaced by an alien-Cole?" Nils said, seemingly unable to resist making a joke. "Sorry, mate, I didn't mean to trivialise how you feel."

Kyra flashed a look, indicating for Nils to keep quiet. "I can see that all of those things are against everything he stood for before the accident, but – you know, the whole experience might just have turned his world upside down."

Lukas took a large swig of his drink and, sighing, poured himself another, slowly shaking his head.

Jess broke the awkwardness. "That on its own does sound pretty lame, but he hasn't made any effort to see Lukas. Plus, as we've said, he and Sofia do seem far more loved-up than we've ever seen them."

"As I've already said, that's not surprising. She probably thought she'd lost him," Kyra said.

"She didn't seem so bothered when she thought he was going to be disabled or had brain damage," Lukas said.

Jess put her hand on Lukas' shoulder. "I've noticed that whenever we're with them and talk about friends that we all know, Sofia always manages to pass some comment that tells Cole where he met them. It's as if she's priming him."

"But that, too, could be down to his amnesia," Kyra said.

Jess nodded, then said to Lukas, "Tell Nils and Kyra what you told me about how he looks at you."

Lukas flashed her an irritated look. "This sounds ridiculous, but when he saw me, when he came out of the coma, the way he looked at me was how he'd look at a stranger. And the way he looks at me now hasn't improved, either." Lukas' voice almost broke as he said, "We loved each other like brothers."

Nils and Kyra looked at each other.

"So, what would you like us to look into?" Nils asked.

"I'm not sure, but when it comes down to it, I know very little about his background. Maybe the accident has stirred up memories, or something. I don't know?"

"Surely you talked about his life previous to uni when you first met?" Kyra asked.

"No, not really. We just hit it off. I know he comes from Liverpool, and that he and Sofia were going out when he started uni, and that his nan brought him up, but apart from that – zilch."

"Okay. We can look into his past. I presume you've got his information from when he joined the firm?" Nils asked.

"Yes, we have."

Kyra looked at Nils before saying, "We'll do what we can. I can start looking into his family and see if there is anything that might be affecting how he is recovering. That's all I can do, okay?"

"Do you think you could find anything about the accident in Africa, or would that be too hard?"

It was Nils that answered this question. "Nothing is impossible."

Lukas went over and hugged them both. "Thank you, both of you. It'll help put my mind at ease, at least."

After a while, the conversation turned to more trivial matters. They continued to drink and listen to music. At one point, Nils demonstrated a dance, using Lukas as his partner, which had the girls dying of laughter.

Well after 2.00 a.m., after Kyra and Nils left, Jess went to bed, and Lukas cleared the glasses away and sat in the lounge. He wondered if he was the one who hadn't been there for Cole. Over the last few years, Lukas had been too involved in his own life, having gone through ups and downs when he'd first met Jess. He felt guilty when he thought back to how he'd reacted when she'd told him about his great-grandfather and the *Aliciana*. And that a ghost had talked to her. But now it was his turn to feel unsettled about Cole. Jess was on solid ground and was behind him one hundred percent. He could turn his attention to his best friend.

The last time Lukas and Cole had seen each other was just before he went out to Ethiopia, and he'd been incredibly happy about going. He loved helping communities gain access to water.

Whatever was going on with his friend, Lukas knew that Nils and Kyra would do their best to help him find and solve the problem.

16

After a very late, leisurely breakfast, Kyra and Nils started to read through the application form Cole had sent in for his job. Lukas had managed to get hold of a copy without any fuss. He'd asked his secretary to email it to him, under the pretence he wanted to check something about Cole's nan. In turn, he'd emailed it to Kyra.

Apart from Cole's date of birth, which they already knew, there was very little family information. The only other name mentioned anywhere was Sofia's, and the most obvious omission was an address for his nan. The name of Cole's secondary school appeared on the form, and Nils and Kyra already knew about his time at university and his degree. The most positive part of his application was his personal statement about why he wanted to work with Andersson Global, citing a desire to work with a company that valued philanthropy alongside monetary gain. A huge list of charities that he already personally supported followed the statement. Kyra thought the best and most useful piece of information – the one that would help them move forward in their search – was knowing which school he'd attended.

Nils stopped reading. "What do you think Lukas is expecting to find out? This whole thing seems a little weird."

"I know. Although it's odd Lukas doesn't know more about Cole's family, there's no real reason why he should. But I don't know what Lukas is thinking at all. Does he think the person who in appearance looks like Cole isn't actually Cole?"

Nils pulled a face at Kyra. "You mean, is he a doppelgänger, or an alien clone?"

"Don't be stupid. Although, the obvious is that Cole is a twin."

"Surely, Sofia would know about a twin, and she'd be able to tell the difference. Wouldn't she?"

"You'd think so. I've never been out with an identical twin, but they must have differences. I'm sure that can't be it."

"Me neither, although I've often fantasised about it." Nils smiled.

"Your brain only ever thinks of one thing!"

Nils continued. "Seriously, though, I think maybe Lukas just has too much money to spend. Maybe if he didn't have money to throw around, he'd accept that the accident changed his friend."

"That's a bit harsh, Nils. Lukas can't make the connection he previously had with Cole, and it's deeply upsetting him. Maybe he has got too much money, but if that's what it takes to settle his unease, then let him pay us to research Cole's background."

They sat in silence for a while, individually searching for Cole's name online, only to find positive articles and reports linked to his name.

Nils suddenly made Kyra jump. "I've had what might seem like an extravagant idea..."

Kyra looked at him expectantly.

Nils continued. "Why don't we go to Africa. Me and Lukas? We could visit the site of the accident and see if there's anything weird about it."

"That's perhaps a little too excessive. How do you think that would help?" Kyra asked.

"Well." Nils paused. "It seems the locals didn't do much investigation on the ground. From what Lukas has told us, and as far as we know, Cole could have got into some trouble out there."

"Like what?"

"I don't know. Maybe he got mixed up in something shady – although from what we've read about him, it's unlikely. He seems to be incredibly honest and caring. We don't seem to have much to go on at this end, do we?"

"That's true, but how are you going to fund it?"

"As I've already said, Lukas has the money. He's worried about his friend, and I think he'd probably do anything that would sort out whatever trouble he's in."

Kyra still felt a little apprehensive about the idea and, she had to admit, a little peeved.

"Why are you going to take Lukas, when you have another journalist who is used to researching?" she asked.

"Erm, I think Ethiopia isn't a particularly safe place for a woman of your beauty to be set free there."

"What's that supposed to mean?" Kyra's hackles were rising.

"Kyra, I'm joking. Though, seriously, I'd feel happier if you were here. Africa isn't always the safest place, and I think where we'd be going is probably not that well equipped when it comes to comfort. Besides, you would be far better placed making enquiries in Liverpool. If I tried to do that, I don't think I'd do as well as you. And Lukas has been to Africa loads of times before with his job."

"Mm, okay. You've convinced me. A little. I do have to agree – foreign correspondent hasn't ever been a top goal in my journalistic career."

Nils stretched over the table from his laptop and kissed her. “I’ll give Lukas a buzz and see what he thinks of my idea.”

17
AUGUST 2023
MANCHESTER & LIVERPOOL

Kyra and Jess had seen Nils and Lukas off on their flight to Ethiopia the night before. The next morning, Kyra made herself a coffee and settled down in front of her laptop. When she'd typed in Cole's date of birth, it'd been easy to find his birth certificate in the General Register Office database. Finding no father on the birth certificate meant instead she searched for information about Cole's mother, only to find that Belinda Drake had died in 2019. Kyra let out a sigh; that would make things harder. From the document, Kyra gained the name of the hospital where he was born. And when she'd read Belinda's death certificate, she'd found that Betty Drake had recorded her death: Belinda's mother. Cole's nan. That meant Kyra now had a name and an address for her. Bingley Road, Anfield, Liverpool.

As a journalist, she knew that she should follow this up, but she also knew from what Lukas had told her that Cole hadn't yet informed his nan about his accident. She didn't want to be the one to tell her, because Lukas had also mentioned that Cole's nan was fragile. And Kyra certainly didn't want to be the person who caused her upset. Especially if Lukas' suspicions were unfounded. Besides, this wasn't a proper journalist job. First and foremost, she was helping out a friend – even if he did pay her expenses.

Kyra already knew from what Lukas had mentioned that Cole never spoke about his home life, apart from his nan. And they couldn't ask Sofia, because that would raise suspicion. Although Lukas and Jess found Cole's reticence to talk about home odd, Kyra didn't, because neither did she. Her parents had split up when she was young, and now both of her parents were dead, so in her mind it didn't leave much to talk about. Her memories belonged to her and Fran; she didn't feel the need to share them with everyone else. Although, she had at least opened up to Nils about her background. But he wasn't everyone.

Kyra continued her search, scanning through the newspapers of 2019 to find out how Belinda Drake had died and was surprised to read a verdict of suicide. Kyra stared at the screen, wondering why on earth she'd kill herself when she had a son studying at university and set for a successful career?

Searching through other local newspapers of the time, she looked for any more news about her death, but couldn't find anything. A complete dead end.

She had to contact Lenny Briggs.

After breakfast the next morning, Kyra searched for Lenny's number in her mobile contacts, hoping he might be able to help. She assumed that he still worked at the *Liverpool Post*, although that was only a guess; he must've been getting on, and he might even have retired. He'd been at the *Post* for years under different guises: sports news, breaking news, and most recently, crime reporter. Over the years he'd built up a huge network of contacts in the area. The good, the bad, the ugly and the downright dangerous.

His phone continued to ring, so she left him a message, asking him to call her back.

About fifteen minutes later, her search through other news outlets from that time was interrupted by her mobile ringing. She saw it was Lenny.

"Hi, Kyra, how you doing?" he said when she answered. "Long time no hear."

Kyra pulled a face at her mobile.

"What can I do for you?" he asked.

"Thanks for getting back to me, Lenny. I'm trying to find some info about someone who grew up in Liverpool, around the Anfield area. But, so far, all I've managed to find is his birth certificate, which doesn't give me an address. His mother's dead – she committed suicide in 2019. I've looked through the newspapers, but can't find anything about it."

"What's the name of the guy you're looking for? Do you know which school he went to?" Lenny asked.

"His name is Cole Drake, and although he did go to school in the area where he lived, several of the schools have closed down. When I tried to get some info, I didn't get far. They'd only set up the new school a year or so before the pandemic and haven't got around to organising the records of pupils who'd left."

"Mm, okay. Well, let me do some asking around the area to see if anyone knows him. What was his mother's name?"

"Belinda Drake – she never married."

"By the way, congratulations on that article about the *Aliciana* scandal. You did some great work there."

Kyra felt pleased he'd heard about it. "Thanks, Lenny."

"Listen, if I find anyone that remembers this Cole, I'll ask them if they'd be happy to talk to you. I'll get back to you in a couple of days."

"Okay. Thanks, Lenny, I appreciate that."

True to his word, a few days later, Lenny phoned back.

"I've found a guy who went to school with Cole. He mentioned that he had a brother and, wait for it...they were twins."

Kyra couldn't believe what she'd just heard. That could explain everything. *I might not have to bother Cole's nan after all.*

"You still there?" Lenny shouted.

"Yeah. Sorry, that's worth knowing and something I hadn't found. I'll go back and look at the birth records. I must have missed it."

"Yeah. You know, if your man was the last baby to be registered on the page, his twin will be on the top of the next page. If they are registered and they're on the same page, twins have the same registration number on their certificate, but if one twin is the last entry on the page, the other twin will have a different registration number—"

Kyra interrupted him. "That's interesting, Lenny, but not particularly relevant to this case. I didn't know he was a twin, so I didn't even think to turn the page. But, thank you that's brilliant that you've confirmed that Cole has a twin brother. Do you think his old school mate will talk to me?"

"Yeah, probably, especially if you buy him a bevvy or two. Do you want his contacts?"

"Please. And thanks, Lenny, that's been incredibly helpful. I might get back to you again, if you don't mind?"

After jotting down the name and number Lenny had sent over, Kyra sat staring at her notepad for some time. So, Cole had a twin brother. *That makes things a lot more interesting.* What if they were identical? Her mind raced with ideas, so she didn't waste any time. She gave Gaz Stevens a buzz and made a date to meet him at a pub in the Liverpool city centre.

Two days later, Kyra travelled over to Liverpool on the train. She arrived as planned, extra early as she'd decided she'd go to Bingley Road. She asked the taxi driver who'd driven her there to wait and got out to talk to an older woman she saw watering a hanging planter on her door.

"Excuse me, I'm sorry to bother you, but have you lived here long?"

The woman looked Kyra up and down.

"Why? What do you want to know?"

"I'm looking for a Betty Drake. Do you know her?"

"Only a little. She moved away just before Covid. I think she went into sheltered housing."

"I don't suppose you know where, do you?"

The woman shook her head.

"Thank you."

Kyra got back into the taxi and asked to be driven into the centre. She knew she didn't need to talk to Cole's nan if what Lenny suggested was true, but part of her also wanted to see where Cole had grown up. Knowing that Betty Drake now lived in care, she definitely didn't want to bother her. She hoped that her meeting with Gaz would reveal more information. Her phone pinged as she received a text from Gaz to say he had arrived at the pub where he'd suggested meeting. He'd included a selfie too. She always found it interesting, meeting up with people, especially when you had no idea what they looked like, so his picture helped.

Gaz looked around the same age as Cole, though she still didn't know if they'd been in the same year group at school or if Gaz just remembered him.

She could have asked her questions over the phone, but she liked to see the people she was talking to, plus while she was in Liverpool, she could go to the central library and search for more local information.

"Thanks for taking the time to meet up with me," Kyra said as she reached the table where he sat. "What can I get you to drink?"

"Erm, a Guinness, ta, love."

Kyra returned with Gaz's Guinness and her own glass of orange; she needed a clear head.

"So, Lenny tells me you want to know about Cole and his brother. What d'ya need to know?"

"Well, how well did you know them? Were you in the same year as them?"

"Yeah. Same class."

"Brilliant. So, are they identical twins?" Kyra prayed they were.

Gaz licked the Guinness froth from his lips. "Like peas in a pod."

Kyra wanted to scream with excitement at that news but managed to contain herself. "And were they alike in temperament?"

Gaz looked a little uncertain.

Kyra rephrased her question. "I mean, were their personalities alike? Did they behave in similar ways?"

"Erm, not really. Cole was a bit of a teacher's pet; a goodie-goodie, and Caleb was a proper scally. Always getting in trouble."

Kyra thought for a moment. "Do you know if they behaved the same outside school? I mean, did Caleb get in trouble then?"

Gaz took a long swig of his beer. "Yeah, you never saw 'em together outside school. Cole'd be at home swotting, and Caleb was just wild." He took another swig, shaking his head, as if recalling a memory. "I mean, that's why Caleb ended up in clink."

"What did he do?"

"Well, from what I remember, he got in with a local gang. Was talk of selling drugs, and then the gang were involved in a robbery where someone was killed. Caleb and some others got nicked, and then they were locked up."

"Do you know where he went to prison?"

"Nah, I didn't keep in touch with them outside school, but everyone was talking about it back then."

"And what about Cole?"

"Well, as I said, he was clever, so he went off to university, but I don't know where or anything."

"Did you know a girl called Sofia at school, possibly Cole's girlfriend?" Kyra asked.

Gaz thought for a while. "Yeah. Yeah, now you mention it. A younger bird, quite a looker, you know, a blonde. I think she was keen on Caleb, but I don't know if they were together. After school, I joined the army for a bit. Then when I came back, most people had moved on." He took another drink. "But I heard a rumour a couple of years back that Caleb was dead."

Kyra's growing hope diminished hearing that one word. She couldn't believe it. If Caleb was dead, that didn't help at all. But still, she did wonder why neither Cole nor Sofia had ever talked about Caleb.

"Thanks so much for what you've told me. Would you like another drink before I go?"

"I'm fine, ta, love. I need to get back to work, anyway."

Kyra walked to the library and found the archive department. She spent the afternoon searching for anything about Caleb Drake's arrest or his subsequent death. The information she found was very sketchy. She read the article about the robbery gone wrong, where a security guard got shot, then a piece about the police arresting several members of the gang who couldn't escape the premises on time. There were only a few names of the main gang members mentioned, but she assumed that was the robbery Gaz had talked about and Caleb was among the unnamed gang members.

Later, she found a tiny article from 2019 about the police finding an abandoned car believed to have been rented and driven by Caleb Drake, 21, who had just been released from Haverigg Prison. His body hadn't been found, and he was therefore presumed dead.

This opened up so many possibilities in Kyra's mind. Maybe Caleb wasn't dead after all. No body – no proof!

18

AUGUST 2023
LIVERPOOL

Lenny knew that if Susie still worked as a Local Intelligence Officer, she would be able to help him get access to files, especially if he bought her a couple of drinks. He'd known her for years. When they'd first met, she'd been a Police Community Support Officer, and he often came into contact with her in his everyday work. One thing he could always rely on with Susie – she could gossip for England. He could always rely on her telling him about the latest news from the station.

They met up in a local pub on the outskirts of the city. She never wanted to meet up near her police station, in case anyone she worked with saw her. Susie's job as an LIO meant that, daily, she had access to sensitive information, which she knew should never be passed on to the press. However, it never seemed to stop Susie from chatting to Lenny about all sorts of things he knew she shouldn't.

After exchanging pleasantries, Lenny asked Susie how hard it would be for her to find him some information. He told her the name he was interested in, saying if she could give him anything, he'd be very grateful.

Susie smiled at him as she downed her third G&T. "You know I'm always pleased to see you, Lenny. Of course, I'll find what I can for you. How's the wife?"

"Fine, thanks. How's..." He couldn't remember her husband's name.

"Oh, I'm on husband number three now. It's a while since I saw you. His name's Jim, and he's a real looker. Younger than me too." Susie gave Lenny a knowing wink.

He'd not been married for years, but never let on to Susie. She seemed to have a voracious appetite when it came to men, and he definitely wanted to steer clear. She had her uses in gathering information for him, but that was it.

"I've got to be getting back to the missus, so do you want another before I go?"

"Oh, that's very kind of you. I'll get that information for you as soon as I can."

After ordering her another drink at the bar and taking it back to her, he made a hasty exit.

A week later, he had a call from Susie, saying she had the information he wanted, and did he want to meet up at the bar again?

When he arrived, Susie had a couple of glasses in front of her – she'd obviously made a head start. After ordering his own beer, and another G&T for her, he sat in the chair opposite to Susie.

"You're going to be so pleased with me. I found your man and all sorts of information!"

She slid a brown envelope over the table towards him. Carefully he took out its contents: a file. He opened it and then shut it quickly, looking around to make sure no one could see or, more importantly, read what he was looking at.

"How the heck did you manage to get this out of the station? Don't they check you when you leave?"

"No, but they don't expect us to have anything. I mean, most of the stuff we see has been filed away for quite a time. Is it any use?"

Lenny sat looking through the document he'd been given. The record of one Caleb Drake who had been arrested in 2016 while taking part in a robbery along with several members of a local gang – The Johnsons. Quite a large part of the document had been crossed out with a thick black marker pen. As he read, he vaguely remembered the case. A security guard had been shot, and they'd caught several of the gang members still on site. He kept reading, and saw that Drake had been released from prison in 2019, but on the day of his release, the car he had been driving had been abandoned by the Irish Sea, with all of his clothes and papers left on the front seat. On the file, someone had written: '*Missing, presumed dead.*'

"Isn't the news what you were hoping for?" Susie asked.

"No, not really, but at least I know what happened to him. Thanks, Susie. You'd better slip this back in tomorrow."

"Anyway, who is this Caleb guy?" she asked.

"Someone wanted me to check on his identity and find out where he is now. Obviously, he's not around, so I think they'll have come to a different decision about their thinking."

Susie took another drink. "You know, when we were teenagers, Tony Johnson went to school with me. I still often see some of his lads about. They think the world of him, because he treats them like family."

Lenny was surprised; he'd not known they'd been at school together. "Did you know he died while still in prison?"

Susie looked genuinely sad. "No. No, I didn't. Oh, he was so good-looking in those days – quite a catch. He seemed okay back then." She smiled wistfully.

Lenny couldn't believe that this woman, getting slowly wasted on G&Ts, worked for the police. He wondered how she'd got through the vetting process for the job, which there must surely have been. But then, maybe she had just moved across from her support officer role, or worse still maybe someone on the inside wanted her there. He decided not to think about the consequences any further. He had the information he wanted and could give Kyra feedback.

He walked away, leaving Susie drinking.

~

"Hi, Kev, fancy seeing you here. I was just telling my friend that I knew some of Tony's lads. Oh, God, I'm so sorry to hear he died."

Kev sat beside her and put his arm around her shoulders.

"So, who have you been chatting to, Susie?"

"A friend, I've known him for years...a journalist."

"Yeah, this friend – what did he want to know?"

"Oh. He was asking about a Caleb Drake. But he found out that he's dead."

Kev removed his arm from Susie's shoulder. "Caleb really is dead, isn't he?" he asked.

"Of course. It says he is missing, presumed dead. It says so in the file." Susie pointed to her bag.

Looking very thoughtful, he asked, "So, didn't they find his body?"

"I don't think so, otherwise it wouldn't say, *'Missing, presumed dead,'* would it?"

"Thanks for the sarcasm, Susie."

Kev kissed her on the cheek before rushing out of the pub, talking on his mobile as he went.

~

Lenny phoned Kyra the day after his meeting with Susie.

She told him her news, that she now knew Cole and Caleb were identical twins, and there were rumours that Caleb was probably dead. However, she hadn't found anything that substantiated that, she said.

In turn, Lenny shared his news, some of which Kyra already knew, but then he told her that he wondered if Caleb had given evidence against the rest of the gang.

"You know, I've been thinking that three years isn't that long for such a serious crime," Kyra said. "You might be right. But surely, he wouldn't want to stay around here after turning evidence? And I don't think the British police get people new identities. That all sounds a bit 'American crime series', doesn't it?" Kyra said.

Lenny answered, "Well, from what I've found out by asking around about the Johnsons, they were a pretty dangerous crew. They had links in Holland with an Organised Crime Group, running drugs, human trafficking – girls for sex and worse. The head guy in Holland is one Marius de Haan. I think the police have been after them for some time, but since Tony Johnson died in prison, things seem to have gone quiet, so a lot of their leads have dried up."

Kyra said, "So, it's unlikely the police would have feigned Caleb's death, but he could have done it himself, or with some help from someone? What do you think?"

"Yeah, but who would help him?"

"Well, I don't think Cole would have. He's never talked about him, and according to Gaz, they didn't spend much time together out of school. And he didn't even tell Lukas, his best friend, that he had a brother." She paused. "And, what's really interesting, Sofia didn't tell Lukas about him, either."

"Who's Sofia?"

"Cole's wife. And according to Gaz, they all knew each other at school, plus he remembers Sofia having a 'thing' for Caleb."

"And she's never mentioned him either?"

"No. Erm, Lenny, do you have any contacts with someone who could tell us the names of visitors Caleb had while he was inside?"

"I'll certainly try."

"Thanks, Lenny, you've found me some great information. Now we just have to find out if Caleb is actually dead, or if he set up his death so he could leave the country."

19
JULY 2023
MANCHESTER

Caleb considered Sofia's question. *Why was he in Africa?*

Looking back, at the time, he'd thought, *Why not?* He'd travelled through Europe before, and during lockdowns, had managed to survive under the radar. When he'd heard of the number of deaths in the UK, he'd needed to know that his brother and Sofia were safe. Obviously unable to be himself, he'd signed on to Facebook as Sam Duncan and had used an image of the sea for his profile photo. Setting up the page, he'd been able to see a lot of Cole's life. He saw that Cole had married Sofia, not long after he'd staged his own demise. At the time, that had angered him to the point where he drank himself silly, but when reason set in, although he felt betrayed, he could understand. Sofia wanted to settle down. And Cole's prospects must have looked good to her.

He'd also been able to see how well Cole's career had progressed, and when he noticed that he was travelling to Ethiopia to do some reconnaissance work, he had the mad idea that he wanted to be able to see Cole, albeit from a distance.

"Caleb, what were you doing in Africa?" Sofia repeated, bringing him back to the moment.

He began to tell the story of how he'd first set foot on the continent in Alexandria, after earning his passage, working as a crew member on a private yacht bound for Egypt. He'd been paid handsomely to deliver some parcels to someone in Cairo, and he'd known by the amount of money he'd earned that they were most likely packets of drugs. He'd spent Christmas in the city before moving on and travelling by bus to Addis Ababa. The journey, although long, had given him a good introduction to the country and its land.

Ethiopia was mostly rural. After leaving Egypt, the scenery they drove through was more varied. There was considerably more greenery, with much of the country being agricultural land, and they passed through mountainous country too. The roads to Addis Ababa were mostly muddy tracks. Gazing out of the bus window, he saw many people walking to local markets, with small herds of goats and people using donkeys as transportation to carry all and sundry.

As he travelled, he got used to seeing the incongruous satellite dishes sitting on top of corrugated iron roofs on the huts he passed. On occasions his heart missed a beat, as there were times the bus careered around bends and then crept along the sections of roads where there were countless hairpin turns. He'd read that there were lots of bus crashes, but most of the time he was enjoying the views too much to overly worry. Though there weren't as many dramatic sights as Egypt, and there were several places where they passed through land that was purely brown and muddy, he thought Ethiopia had a beauty all of its own.

Sofia continued to listen, but after a while, asked, "So when did you see Cole?"

"I'm getting there, but I need to tell you about Megasu first."

He'd met Megasu in a bar not far from his hotel in Addis. Caleb made the mistake of ordering a chai buna, which he thought sounded pretty good. It turned out to be a mix of tea and coffee together, in the same cup, and it was disgusting. Megasu watched Caleb as he tried his drink, and burst out laughing at the face he pulled on his first sip. That started their conversation, and Megasu suggested that if Caleb brought him a beer too, he'd introduce him to the best available. They were soon chatting over glasses of Harar beer and talking about football. To his surprise, Caleb heard that serious fights had broken out over Arsenal and Manchester United games. Megasu was an Arsenal supporter, which surprised Caleb. He explained to Megasu that he supported Liverpool because he'd grown up near the ground. They agreed to meet the next day, when Megasu would show Caleb around the sights of Addis. When he invited him to his home, in Gedo, north west of Addis, Caleb felt he couldn't say no.

Despite the age of Megasu's car, it managed the long journey well. Arriving in Gedo, Caleb was introduced to more Ethiopian customs and a variety of foods, and he enjoyed the company of his newfound friend.

One day, when Caleb had been living in Gedo for around three months, he'd gone up to Goda Gora. On that fateful day, Cole spotted him – and everything went sideways. Sadly, from the off, they automatically fell back into their love—hate relationship. They argued about almost everything.

"Cole had been taken out for a birdwatching trip – a sort of 'jolly'—"

"A what?" Sofia interrupted.

"Yeah, a birdwatching trip. You won't believe it, but it's a big thing in Ethiopia. They even have entire holiday itineraries based on birdwatching, and the Ethiopians often arrange for visiting business people to go on these trips too.

"So, Cole was being driven back to Gedo by his driver, Abdi, and as they were travelling through Goda Goro, Cole saw me, and told Abdi to stop. Cole called out my name, and despite having lived as 'Sam' for the last few years, I instantly recognised his voice and automatically turned around. After an awkward exchange, he persuaded me to go back to his hotel in Gedo with him for a drink. I wasn't sure about it and less certain that I wanted to travel in the open-sided safari jeep. I'd have expected him to be driven around in a much smarter vehicle. Anyway, I'd asked Megasu, my travelling companion to follow behind, keeping a slight distance in case I lost it with Cole and got out. Megasu would be able to pick me up and we could continue our journey.

"As we sat in the back of the old jeep, I don't think either of us had even noticed there were no seatbelts. In fact, there was little evidence to suggest there had ever been any fitted. Abdi drove recklessly along the bumpy mud road, while Cole and I clung onto the seats in front of us, shouting above the noise of the engine.

"We started to argue almost as soon as we got into the jeep. He couldn't believe I'd lied about my death, and the amount of hurt I'd caused everyone. I can still remember most of our argument. Cole said something along the lines of: 'You've always been the same. I don't know why I'm so surprised. You've always been incredibly selfish and stupid. I mean, why on earth did you get involved with those people, anyway? You could have got yourself a decent job. You're an intelligent man.'

"I sat staring ahead, listening to the same old rhetoric he'd always thrown at me. He always managed to make me feel like a failure.

"'You didn't have to speak to me today, you know. You could just have carried on with your perfect little life. I suppose it is perfect, isn't it?' I asked him.

"'It's pretty good, yes,' Cole answered. 'I don't know how you'll feel about this – I don't know if you heard, but Sofia and I are married.'

"'Yes, I know,' I said. 'You didn't wait long to get in there, did you?'

"Cole didn't answer. So, I asked him: 'Why didn't any of you come and visit me in prison?'

"'Nan didn't want me to,' he said. 'She didn't want me to ruin my chances at college, and Sofia and I only got together when she thought you were dead.'

"I think I said something about him being a *nanny's boy*, which made him even more annoyed. 'So, when did you start seeing Sofia?' I asked.

"'I just told you, when we thought you'd killed yourself. She was inconsolable.'

"'Obviously not.'

"Then Cole mentioned our mum killing herself, because she'd heard about my death. That really angered me, and even though we'd already been arguing, that's when the argument took on an even worse tone. We were almost screaming at one another.

"Abdi had decided to take a shortcut, which he thought would make our journey quicker. Probably he wanted to get it over too, rather than have these two men in the back of his jeep yelling at each other. His quicker route was basically a mud track that had incredible twists and winding turns. Eventually, there came a point where we were going far too fast for the road. He took a bend at high speed, skidded as the wheels hit a deep pothole, and completely lost control. As the jeep bounced and rolled, I lost hold of the seat I'd been clinging to, and was thrown from the car. I don't remember what happened after that, until I heard Megasu calling my name. He told me later that as he'd careered around the bend, a scene of carnage had greeted him.

"I eventually came to, and gradually through my fuzzy brain, heard his stricken voice calling out, '*Ato* Sam! Sam—'"

Sofia interrupted again. "What's *Ato* mean?"

"Oh, *'mister'*.

"I came to," Caleb said, continuing his story, "feeling sick, with an excruciating pain in my body, so much so it hurt to breathe. Slowly, I managed to make sense of what Megasu was saying. 'Sam? Are you okay, Sam?' I tried to sit up, but instantly felt violently sick again. Megasu told me to keep still.

"Trying to speak, I could only manage a hoarse whisper, and asked: 'Where's my brother?' Megasu had to ask me to repeat what I'd said.

"After I did, he looked at me strangely. 'Your brother?'

"I explained there was a man that looked like me – identical.

"I heard the sound of Megasu's feet moving slowly, as he walked away searching for Cole, then he returned much quicker a few seconds later, looking shocked. 'The driver's dead, sprawled across the bonnet with his head at a very strange angle to his body. And the other man, your brother – he's dead. He does look just like you.'

"I remember thinking I hadn't seen my brother in seven years, and the last thing we'd done was argue.

"Megasu said he'd get help. That was when, despite my pain, or maybe because of it, I had this terrible, desperately twisted thought. An idea that could improve my life by one hundred percent. A way for me to go home."

Caleb looked sideways to see Sofia's response. She had her hand over her mouth. He continued.

"I asked Megasu to go and get everything from my brother's pockets and bring it to me. He gave me a strange look, but did as I asked. Returning, he bent down to show me what he'd found: Cole's wallet, a hotel room key, and his mobile phone.

"I asked Megasu if Cole was wearing a watch or a ring, and if so, could he remove them and bring them to me? He disappeared a second time, then returned with Cole's watch and the gold wedding band.

"By then, the feeling of dizziness had increased and I wondered how much longer I could remain conscious. But the thought that I could go home gave me the strength to give orders.

"God forgive me, I explained what I was going to do and asked Megasu to hide Cole's body in the bush, hoping that hyenas would find him."

Caleb heard Sofia gasp, but he carried on with his tale.

"Next, I asked him to put the gold band on my finger, remove my watch, and replace it with Cole's. I told him to drop the wallet and mobile near where I lay so it would look as though they'd fallen out of my jeans as I'd been thrown from the jeep. I told him that he could keep my watch and take my wallet plus any money inside, but that he must throw my mobile and burn my documents.

"Megasu looked at me strangely. He couldn't understand at all why I wanted to go home as Cole rather than myself. It was far too complicated to explain, and I was in so much pain, it took me all my strength to think.

"I thanked him, telling him I'd miss him, but whatever happened, most importantly, he had to pretend he didn't know me. Reluctantly, Megasu agreed."

Caleb hadn't been able to look at Sofia while he'd told this part of the story. Now he glanced at her and saw silent tears flowing down her cheeks. He reached out and gently brushed them away. He looked at her, a glance that asked if he should continue. Sofia nodded.

Caleb took a deep breath. "I don't remember much more, apart from flashes of colour, muffled voices, strange sounds and pain as I continually faded in and out of consciousness during my journey back to Manchester. In fact, I don't remember anything about being flown home at all. I think the paramedics who'd flown from the UK gave me drugs that knocked me out completely.

"Megasu had always excelled when it came to following instructions, so I knew he'd do exactly what I asked him.

"You know some of the rest, though I had to ask Lukas some of the detail when I came out of my coma. He explained that a local man – I knew he was talking about Megasu – had helped the police put me, and Abdi's body, into their vehicle and they'd driven me to a local medical centre. They're not really medical centres in our meaning of the word. They lack any real medical equipment or trained staff. When they saw how seriously hurt I was, they contacted the hotel in Addis, from the number on the room key, and in turn they'd ended up getting in touch with Andersson Global, who arranged for me to be flown home."

Caleb didn't dare look at Sofia again. She made the first move. Shuffling further along the sofa, she curled up with her head in his lap. He gently lifted her up into his arms, and they remained clinging on to each other, in that same position for some time. Caleb had to come face-to-face with his demons. And he expected that Sofia had demons of her own to face.

Caleb wondered if Sofia had fallen asleep, but a little later, she pulled away from him.

Looking into his eyes, she said, "I'm sad Cole's dead, but you did the only thing you could, and if you hadn't, I wouldn't have had either of you."

He wasn't sure if that was a good thing, until she kissed him and whispered, "I love you, Caleb."

20

AUGUST 2023

ETHIOPIA

Lukas and Nils had landed in Addis Ababa at 12.40 p.m. It'd taken them some sixteen hours to fly there from Manchester, and they'd both felt drained when they'd arrived, so they'd decided to have a good rest and shower before meeting up to chat about the next few days.

During the flight, Lukas had talked about Cole's job, explaining to Nils what he would have been doing during his time in Ethiopia. His dad had already been in touch with Mahmoud, the company's contact in Addis, who knew the rather sketchy details about Cole's accident. Mahmoud was going to arrange transport for them to Gedo, and he would organise someone to meet them on the ground who could help them try to find leads about what happened to Cole. Even though the accident had occurred three months earlier, Lukas knew life in Ethiopia moved at a slower pace than in Europe, and his dad had said Mahmoud was confident they should be able to find something tangible.

Lukas ambled along to Nils' room and knocked on the door, until eventually, Nils appeared, wrapped in a large towel.

"I'm sorry, I fell asleep for quite some time, then got chatting to Kyra, and I've only just got out of the shower, as you can see." Nils laughed and did a twirl in his towel. "Come in. It won't take me long to get dressed."

Lukas went into Nils' room and couldn't believe how tidy it looked. Back in his room, his suitcase lay open on his bed with clothes half in, half out where he'd rifled through to find what he wanted to wear. He was going to clear it up when he got back. After all, they were going to leave their main stuff in their rooms and just take a rucksack with them when they travelled to the accident area. He couldn't help but comment on Nils' neatness.

"Okay. Have you been talking to Kyra?" Nils said from the bathroom.

Lukas shook his head then added, "No" as he realised Nils couldn't see him.

"Well, she calls me a *neat freak*, because she thinks I'm overly tidy."

"I don't know that anyone can be overly tidy, but"—and Lukas looked around the room again — "compared to my room, I'd have to agree with her. You are a neat freak!"

Nils walked in from the bathroom, minus the towel, completely naked. "You're supposed to be on my side." He got himself dressed, while Lukas stood looking out at the view from his room window.

"This view is amazing, isn't it?"

Nils laughed. "What, better than watching me get dressed? I forget, I'm so used to walking around naked at home. I did the same in Kyra's place, and then her sister walked in."

"She'll just put it down to you being Swedish," Lukas replied.

"Oh, Fran wasn't the slightest bit embarrassed. She's a nurse, though I suppose you know that?"

"Yeah. To be honest, I can't imagine many things that would embarrass her." Lukas smiled.

“Anyway, I thought we’d go for a walk, get some fresh air, come back for drinks. Then I’m taking you out for a meal.”

“Is where we’re eating a surprise?”

“Yep, but you’ll enjoy it.”

They walked around the grounds of the hotel, and then crossed over the main road, into Ethiopia Park, before returning to the hotel bar. Over drinks, Nils updated Lukas with Kyra’s news that she was going to meet up with her old journalist friend from Liverpool, and Lukas mentioned that Jess had met Sofia and Cole out in Manchester, and according to her, they were still both very loved-up.

Out of the blue, Nils said, “Hey, I just read about the history of Ethiopia on the flight. There’s so much I didn’t know, but I was surprised to find they are one of only two African nations not to have been colonised by Europeans. Did you know that?”

“Yes, though not until Dad told me. That’s why when you speak to them, not surprisingly, they are very proud of being Ethiopian. They’ve actually ousted the Italians twice—”

“So I read. That’s amazing.”

“And because there were Italians who stayed on, they introduced their food, and Ethiopians love Italian food!”

“Seriously?”

“So, you’ve ruined my surprise, but that’s what we’re eating tonight. I’ve booked a table at Castelli’s restaurant,” Lukas said. “The first time I came here, Dad took me. The meals at Castelli’s are something to experience! It’s said to be one of the best Italian restaurants in the world.”

A little later, they travelled the short journey by taxi to Castelli’s. Lukas watched Nils’ reaction when they entered the restaurant. “What you expected?” he asked.

“Not sure. It’s very old-fashioned in style, but—” Nils stopped mid-sentence as he caught site of some of the framed photos hanging on the walls. “It’s obviously been very popular over the years." He took a close look at the images of a young Brad Pitt and Angelina Jolie, Bob Geldof and even US president, Jimmy Carter. "We're eating in some interesting company."

The next morning, following a light breakfast, they were picked up by Mahmoud. He'd arranged for Kofi, the helicopter pilot who'd flown Cole out to Gedo to fly them too.

On the flight, Lukas asked Kofi if he'd noticed Cole being in a bad mood or if he'd seemed at all anxious. But Cole had been very chatty, he said, and was full of anticipation about his trip. In fact, very positive.

Before leaving Lukas and Nils, Kofi sent his good wishes to Cole for his recovery. Lukas made a note to himself to pass them on, wondering how likely it would be that Cole would remember the pilot's name.

Lukas wanted to see Nils' reaction when they landed in Gedo. After spending so much time travelling around Africa – first with his dad and then on his own for business – Lukas had become used to the vast differences in how people lived compared to in Europe. He expected Nils might experience culture shock.

They were met by Ajani, someone Mahmoud had organised to show them around and take them to the places that Cole had visited. First, he took them to the hotel Cole had stayed in, and where they would also stay: Mida Qanyi. Nils looked a little shocked by their hotel, which looked more akin to a men's hostel back in Europe.

"This is the real Africa, Nils. Not what you probably imagined, but this is reality."

"I didn't know quite what to expect. Despite all the years I've worked in journalism, this is the first time I've visited Africa. It's maybe more basic than I had imagined, but I didn't think I'd have the normal mod-cons, either, so I think I'll cope."

Despite having been in this country many times, Lukas still found it shocking how the majority of people lived – without access to fresh water, and with very poor sanitation. Even in their hotel, they had limited use of water.

"Ajani will take care of us. It will be great to have someone who can speak the local languages. Most people speak Amharic, some speak their own regional language, and many do speak English. So, we'll have it covered between us."

Later, Ajani took them to a local café where Lukas introduced Nils to Harar. Nils was surprised to hear that it was a Heineken brew.

While drinking their beers, Ajani answered questions about Cole's driver, Abdi, who'd died in the crash. According to Ajani, Abdi was one of the company's best drivers, so they were surprised by the accident.

Ajani told them that the next day they'd set off early and travel to the area where Cole had been taken on his birdwatching trip, then on the return journey they could stop along the way at some of the small villages, showing his photograph to see if anyone remembered him. It seemed a pretty laborious way to work, but unlike the UK, they couldn't email all the local police and ask them if they could share the photo in their community. Plus, the government had banned access to social media platforms, so they couldn't even share photos on Facebook. However, even when systems were working, the majority of the population didn't have access, anyway.

Lukas, Nils and Ajani spent the evening devouring a traditional Ethiopian meal of zilzil tibs and injera bread. Lukas always enjoyed the communal style of eating – using your right hand to dip the bread into the sauce and then scooping up the chopped meat.

As planned, the next day they set off with Ajani, who drove them to where Cole had been on his birdwatching trip. They travelled back towards Gedo, and stopped each time they came across a small town or community to show Cole's photo, asking if anyone recognised him.

For most of the morning, no one showed any recognition of seeing him, but around mid-day, they stopped in Goda Goro. A young Ethiopian busy carving wooden animals looked up when they approached him. He stopped his work and gazed at the photo.

He spoke Amharic, according to Ajani, who excitedly translated. "He says that the man is Ato Sam, a friend of Megasu."

Lukas asked, "Does he know where Megasu is at the moment?"

"He's not sure, but he knows he's due in the café later this afternoon."

"Please thank him and give him this for his time." Lukas handed Ajani some cash for the young carver.

They arrived at the café the man had mentioned, and after ordering some food and drink, asked the owner to tell them when Megasu arrived.

Luckily, none of them were in a great rush, because Megasu didn't turn up until about two hours later. He came over to their table, after the owner had told him they wanted to speak to him. Ajani spoke to him in his own language and then introduced Lukas and Nils in English.

Lukas found a picture of Cole in his phone and showed it to Megasu. "Do you know this man?" he asked.

Megasu seemed a little hesitant, but answered, "Yes."

"Please, sit and join us. Would you like a drink?" Lukas asked.

"A beer please."

Pointing at the picture on his phone again, Lukas asked, "Who is he to you?"

"Ato Sam? We were friends, but he left earlier this year." Megasu hesitated, appearing reluctant to say more.

"Did he have an accident?"

Megasu took a long while to answer. "It's complicated, sir."

"Complicated?" Nils said. "How is it complicated? He was either in an accident, or he wasn't."

Megasu took a long sip of the beer that Ajani had placed in front of him.

"We were visiting another friend here in Goda Goro and we were walking along the street. Someone called out to Sam, though I didn't see who it was. As soon as Sam saw this other man, he looked shocked. He told me he would travel back with him in his jeep, asking me to follow behind. I couldn't follow too closely, because of the large blinding cloud of dust the jeep created.

"After about twenty minutes' driving, I came around a bend and had to slam my brakes on. The jeep had crashed into a tree. The driver had gone through the window screen, and at first sight, I could tell he was dead. I panicked, because at first, I couldn't see Sam. I called out his name, and then I found him. His injuries looked severe, and I thought he would die—"

Lukas interrupted his description.

"What about the other man in the jeep? What happened to him?"

"Strangely, I couldn't see the other man to start with, but when I found him, he looked just like Sam. But dead." Megasu took a long drink of his beer, his hand shaking as he held the glass.

"There wasn't any information about another body when the police brought Sam back from the crash. Why not? Didn't they find him?" Lukas asked.

Megasu answered slowly and quietly. "That's because Sam asked me to hide the other man's body."

"Why would you do that?" Lukas asked.

Megasu again took his time answering. "Because Sam was my friend, and he had made a decision that he needed my help with."

Lukas stared at Megasu for some time before asking, "So, what did you do with the body?"

"I dragged the other man's body into the bush, a good way from the accident. Scrubbed out the drag marks with a tree branch that I then tossed into a ditch. I checked inside the car, to remove any evidence of two passengers, which luckily, there wasn't. Then I sat with Sam until help arrived."

"Did Sam tell you to do anything else?" Nils asked, as Lukas found himself unable to speak.

Megasu shook his head. "No. Initially, I hadn't been sure I would do as he asked. It didn't feel right, but then Sam explained to me why he'd asked me to hide the body. Considering the man was already dead, I couldn't have hurt him any more, whereas Sam's injuries were serious and I needed to help him. Get him to safety."

"Didn't you think it odd, though?" Nils urged.

Again, Megasu took his time to answer.

"Yes, but that was the strange thing. I could see Sam's turmoil about the choices he'd made. Of course, upset by his brother's death, but then at the same time, he seemed relieved. I didn't understand why, though."

"Had you known he had a twin brother before that day?" Nils asked.

Megasu shook his head.

Lukas found his voice again and asked, "Are you sure Sam didn't tell you to do anything else?"

Megasu shifted from foot to foot.

"He asked me to get anything that the dead man had on him

in terms of his identity. His mobile, his ring – any personal things."

"What did you do with Sam's papers and mobile?"

"He told me to destroy his paperwork and mobile, but that I could keep his money." He took another quick drink. "But, I couldn't get rid of his phone. I took the sim card out, but I kept it for the photos. I'd known him for several months and we'd become good friends."

Nils looked at his watch. "We've only got an hour or two before it's dark. Do you want to go and see where the accident happened, Lukas?"

"Yes. You're going to take us, Megasu. Okay?"

Apprehensively, Megasu nodded.

They left the café and went to their car, suggesting that Megasu sat in the front so he could direct.

On arrival at the accident site, as Lukas looked at the rough, uneven mud road, he wasn't at all surprised that the accident had happened. The potholes and ruts should have been easy for a jeep to navigate, but if Abdi had lost his concentration, it would have been easy to lose control. One of the tyres could easily have blown.

Ajani parked where Megasu indicated.

"So where did you put the body of Sam's twin?" Nils asked.

Megasu looked around, as though he'd forgotten, though Lukas thought he was probably playing for time.

"Come on, you must remember, or do you often hide bodies?" Lukas asked.

"No, sir, I don't, but it looks a little different now." He wandered around and then walked into the scrubland, then eventually stopped. "I think this is the place."

Lukas and Nils walked to where Megasu stood and began to

look around. Lukas didn't know what he expected to find, but he carefully looked behind some of the bushes. He saw Nils bend down; he tried hard to pull something from under a rock.

"What have you found, Nils?"

"I think it might be a human femur, but it's lodged under here."

Lukas rushed over to try to help. "Careful, we don't want to break it."

Between them and with the help of Ajani, they manage to get the bone free of the rock.

Megasu looked away into the distance.

After examining the bone Nils held in his hand, Lukas turned away to be violently sick. Ajani handed him a bottle of water. Recovering, he said, "Sorry. I didn't expect that. It might not even be Cole's, but what if it is?"

Nils answered. "Well, we have a fifty–fifty chance, so we can take it home. If we ask for your dad's help, we don't have to worry about customs, and then once back in the UK, we can get the DNA tested."

Megasu asked Lukas, "Who was this man to you?"

"Cole. My best friend. I'd never met his twin brother. In fact, I didn't know he had one until coming to Ethiopia. So, your Sam must be Cole's twin, and he is now living my friend's life back in the UK."

"I'm sorry about your friend, sir, but I'm glad my friend Sam is okay."

"I'm not sure he's going to remain okay, Megasu. Impersonating someone else is an offence, so he won't be so happy when we prove he's not Cole."

"Even if it's his twin and he had no part in his death?" Megasu asked.

Lukas glared at him.

Nils wrapped the bone in his jacket and put it in his shoulder bag.

They dropped Megasu back in the town and drove back to their hotel in Gedo. Once there, Lukas and Nils wrapped the bone inside a clean shirt and put it into a plastic bag that Nils just happened to have in his luggage.

"We were lucky finding this," Nils said. "If it wasn't for the incredibly dry conditions, we probably wouldn't have. Let's hope it is Cole's. A horrible thing to hope, but you know what I mean."

Lukas tried to ring Jess but couldn't get through, so Nils tried Kyra, but had the same problem. They decided they'd wait until they got back to Addis before telling them the news.

21

AUGUST 2023
MANCHESTER

Sofia leant over and kissed Caleb before getting out of bed. "I'll see you later," she said. "I'm just going into town to get a few things for our holiday."

"Okay, don't spend too much."

Sofia watched Caleb turn over, and by the time she'd had her shower and dressed, he'd fallen asleep. She'd noticed that he slept more than normal but put it down to the residue of the anaesthetic and medication he'd been on. It was clearly still having an impact on him all these weeks later.

She smiled down at him before setting off to the shops to buy a new bikini and sun hat. Her drawers and wardrobe were full of a huge variety of summer clothes, but her bikini looked very 'last year' and she wanted to look good on the beach.

After a successful time shopping, she returned to find Caleb doing sit-ups in the lounge.

"What the hell are you doing, babes? You're supposed to be careful with your leg. That's what the doctor said."

"I know, but, I'm just trying to get a bit fitter. I don't like sleeping so much. Besides, my leg's fine. I'm not putting much pressure on it. Don't fuss. So, have you spent loads of money? Show me what you got."

Sofia put on the gorgeous sun hat she'd bought. It was very stylish, with a wide brim, perfect to keep the sun off her face and prevent damage to her skin. Then she held up the bikini for Caleb to see.

"Is it worth wearing that?" He laughed. "Put it on. Let me see what it looks like."

"Not now. I know you. It won't stay on for long once you see it. It's not for swimming in – just lying around the pool." She put the tiny strapless two-piece back in the bag. "I bumped into Jess earlier. She said Nils and Lukas have gone out to Ethiopia."

"Did she say why?"

"No, but I think it must be something to do with the accident, mustn't it? There's nothing they can find, is there?"

"No, Sofe, don't worry. Look, what are they going to find? I mean, they don't know I was there. And if they did, how would people know it was me rather than Cole?"

"What about the guy you were friends with – he wouldn't give you away, would he?"

"Megasu – no. No, he won't tell them anything. I mean, what could he tell them? He'd be in trouble too. He'll keep quiet."

Sofia couldn't help but be concerned. Caleb didn't sound totally convinced that Megasu would keep quiet. Different scenarios started to rush around inside her head. "What if they found something of Cole's?"

Caleb sighed before saying, "What are they going to find, huh? If they did, it won't matter, anyway. We're identical twins. We have the same DNA, the same fingerprints, so they won't be able to prove anything. Stop worrying." He smiled at her, trying to reassure her. "The only person who could give us away is Nan, and I'm not going to visit her anytime soon. As long as we stick together, everything'll be fine."

He went over to her and pulled her into his arms. "Are you sure you don't fancy modelling your bikini for me?" He kissed her and started to undo her jeans. "Come on, Sofe, I'll soon make you forget your worries."

All her anxieties and resolve to confront him melted away as her whole being craved his touch.

After they'd made love, Sofia did feel calmer, but not for long. The idea of Lukas and Nils digging around in Ethiopia and finding out what had happened to Cole kept niggling at her. Surely, there was a way that people could tell the difference between identical twins. She knew his nan could, but then she thought back to when they were at school. On the times Cole and Caleb wore the same clothes, no one could tell them apart. She remembered how they often used to swap places for lessons or events where they didn't want to take part. Cole's maths skills were far better than Caleb, and he was far better at English, so they often used to swap places to cause the teachers hassle. Poor Mr Robson, the maths teacher, couldn't understand why Cole suddenly struggled so badly at a subject when he was normally an A-star student!

But the negative thoughts wouldn't go away. What if Nils and Lukas offered Megasu money? Would he turn on his friend then? And what if she couldn't continue to keep up the façade and Lukas found out that his suspicions were right after all and his best mate wasn't who he was supposed to be?

"Caleb, what would you do if Lukas asked you outright if you're Cole?"

"For Christ's sake, Sofia. Let it go, will you? You're getting on my nerves now. How can he be sure? To everyone else, I am Cole.

As long as you keep your nerve, no one ever has to know any different."

Sofia could feel tears beginning to well up. She tried not to cry, but this was the first time Caleb had ever raised his voice at her. Not wanting him to see her tears, she walked away from him, went into the bathroom, and locked the door.

What am I doing? She had welcomed Caleb back with open arms, when all of her old feelings for him had resurfaced. But in reality, she didn't know him, not like she'd known Cole. He'd never shouted at her, not even when she'd done really stupid things. Both she and Caleb had been kids when they'd first been lovers. God knows what he had done in the years between then and now. Tears streamed down her face as she slid down the wall and sat on the tiled floor, quietly sobbing to herself.

She must have been in the bathroom for longer than she'd thought. Caleb began gently knocking on the door.

"Sofe, are you okay?"

Sofia turned the tap on and dabbed cold water over her red eyes. Taking a deep breath to control her breathing, she answered. "Yes, I'll be out in a mo, babes."

Looking at herself in the mirror, she grimaced. She looked a mess. She shook her hair and patted cold water over her face for a second time, and after drying herself, unlocked the door.

Caleb stood outside, leaning against the wall.

"I'm so sorry, Sofe. I didn't mean to be short-tempered with you. I hadn't realised when I took Cole's place just how emotionally draining it would be. Stupidly, I thought it would be easy."

Sofia stared at him.

"Easy, because I hadn't accounted for you. I hadn't factored into the equation that I would fall in love with you all over again."

Sofia started to cry again. "You love me. You really do? You're not just saying it?"

Caleb reached out and pulled her into his arms. "No, I do, truly, love you. I'm sorry that I've put you in this position, having to lie for me, and I'm sorry I just got annoyed with you. It's just so much harder than I'd imagined it would be, pretending to be Cole."

"I'm sorry for being such a snivelling wreck. I hadn't thought about how hard it must be for you, either. I can't help being scared. I don't want to lose you again. I can't lose you again!"

22

2015
ANFIELD, LIVERPOOL

Sofia left home with one of her favourite outfits hidden in her bag. She would change once she arrived at Kat's, because if her dad had seen what she intended to wear, he would have gone ballistic.

At Kat's house, Sofia poured her way into a pair of very tight cut-off jeans then put on a top that wasn't really more than a tiny triangle of material. Basically, it wrapped around her boobs, had one thin strap that tied around her neck and then another even thinner tie that went around her back. She felt very sexy in it and she was all set for getting off with Caleb Drake, who she'd had eyes on for weeks. He was a trouble-maker, but he lived life to the full, and she was excited for him to notice her.

The booming beat of the music could be felt through the walls and floors of the whole house. Sofia and Kat gyrated in the middle of the room hoping to be noticed. Looking around, Sofia saw Caleb nonchalantly leaning against the wall, looking even fitter than he did at school – if possible. He stared straight at her, following her every move. She told Kat she was going to get a drink and sashayed past Caleb, purposefully bumping into him. Giving him her best smile, saying “Sorry” as she passed.

He followed her into the kitchen, and coming up behind her, stretched around her body to get himself a drink, and then asked her, “What you drinking?”

She told him she was drinking vodka, and she thought it made her look more sophisticated than drinking the lager that most of her friends drank.

He poured some for her and asked, “You with anyone?”

“I am now,” she said.

He smiled, a slightly lopsided smile, and taking her hand, he led her into the dark room where people were dancing.

Holding their drinks in one hand, with their arms circled around each other’s waists, they moved on the spot to the music.

They continued dancing for a while until everyone invaded the space to dance to a faster, louder, track.

Moving out of the room, Caleb pulled her after him. He led her through the kitchen, stopping to re-fill her paper cup with vodka and grabbing himself another beer, before going outside into the garden.

As Sofia followed Caleb along the path, she remembered how, on her first visit, she’d been surprised how big Kat’s garden looked compared to her own, even noticing how many plants and bushes there were.

Unexpectedly grabbing her hand, Caleb pulled her behind an extra-large bushy plant and into the shadows. The music, just an indistinct bumping beat, played in the background, and apart from the light from the kitchen, the garden was in complete darkness. Sofia leant against Caleb, pressing herself into his body as their mouths met in a kiss. She couldn’t believe it. She was here, with him. The boy she’d wanted all these weeks and now here they were. His kisses were so hot she could hardly breathe. He ran his hands over her breasts and then up inside her top until she gasped in excitement.

Suddenly he stopped and asked, "How old are you?"

"What does that matter?"

"It does if you're too young."

Sofia lied. She didn't want to tell him she was fifteen. She told him she was old enough, and on the pill – which was true. Even if she hadn't been, she would have lied about that too. She certainly wasn't going to miss the chance of getting laid by the one boy in the school who she fancied the pants off.

They continued kissing and heavily petting. But Sofia knew she'd had too much to drink. The vodka was evidently stronger than she'd thought it would be, and it began to affect her.

Initially she felt a little dizzy, then much to her embarrassment, she had to quickly pull away from Caleb to theatrically vomit. But rather than leave her in disgust, he held her hair away from her face and continued to hold on to her while she emptied her stomach behind the shrub in Kat's parents' garden.

When she finished being sick, he went into the kitchen and got her some water and brought back some kitchen roll for her to clean herself.

"Are you okay?"

She nodded, turning away from him, embarrassed he'd seen her in this state.

"Don't worry, I shouldn't have given you so much to drink. Do you want me to take you home?"

This really surprised Sofia; she thought he would think her a silly little girl who couldn't hold her drink. She thought she'd embarrassed him.

"Thanks. You could but I'm staying over at Kat's tonight."

"Okay. I'm going, but I'll see you soon."

He left, and Sofia spent the rest of the night crying over Kat, bemoaning the fact she'd managed to ruin everything.

A few days later, much to her amazement, Caleb walked over to her as she left school to ask her around to his house that night. She couldn't believe her luck.

The story she told her dad was a lie about going to help Kat with her homework. Again, camouflaging her real outfit, she wore a sloppy jumper over skinny jeans. As soon as she was out of sight of her house, she removed her top to reveal a tight, low cut T-shirt, which is how she looked when she arrived at Caleb's.

To her surprise, an older lady opened the front door, who after looking her up and down, yelled for Caleb to come downstairs and see his friend. He arrived a few seconds later, short of breath, seemingly almost as soon as the woman had finished shouting.

"Hi, good to see you. Come on up."

Sofia had followed him up to his bedroom, which wasn't tidy, but also not the mess that she'd expected. He motioned for her to sit on the bed and asked if she'd like a coffee, then disappeared back downstairs to make it – she presumed.

After he left, she looked around his room. The walls were plastered with photos of footballers and athletes, mostly people she didn't recognise. He had a small TV in one corner and a speaker next to it, and a pile of other techy stuff she had no interest in.

Caleb returned with two coffees and sat next to her on the bed.

Sofia for once was lost for words. She still couldn't quite believe that he'd got back to her, particularly after her drunken act at the party. Caleb chose some music on his phone, Bluetoothed it to his speakers, and soon the track filled the room.

They started kissing, and pretty quickly that led to the best sex she'd ever had – which wasn't saying much, because her observation so far had been that boys had no idea about how to make a girl feel good. Although only a couple of years older than her, Caleb Drake had skills and knew exactly how to make a girl experience complete ecstasy.

Afterwards, Caleb covered them both in his duvet and held her close. Sofia worried whether anyone else in the house had heard them.

"It's not a problem. Nan hasn't got the best of hearing, and when I've got my music playing, it's even harder for her," Caleb said.

"Do you live with your nan, then?"

"Yeah, we have since we were quite little."

"Where's Cole? Is he at home, too?"

"No, he's probably out at the library. He's swotting up all the time. He wants to go to university, so he wants to make sure he passes his exams."

Sofia felt relieved, although slightly surprised at his nan's laid-back approach to parenting. Her dad would never let her and a boy be in her bedroom together. Certainly not out of his earshot.

After that night, they'd become inseparable, and Sofia had spent more time at his nan's house than at her own. She'd felt safer there. Her dad, the person she wanted to get away from, incredibly didn't seem to notice her absence. Out of sight, out of mind.

Sofia knew she loved Caleb. Apart from the odd occasions that he went out with his mates, they were rarely apart. They had amazing sex, and they enjoyed being together. They talked for hours, watched films and listened to music.

Things seemed to be going well, but then he made a new

friend, and gradually she began to see less and less of him. As this new friendship grew, their relationship started to cool, leaving Sofia devastated.

A year later, she heard he was dead. It seemed that, at the age of sixteen, her life had ended.

23
AUGUST 2023
MANCHESTER

Kyra's phone had died, and when she turned it on again, she found a whole load of missed calls from Jess.

"What's up?"

"Kyra, I haven't heard from Lukas, and I can't get hold of him. Have you heard from Nils?"

Kyra could hear the rising panic in Jess' voice. "No, I've not heard, but I know that sometimes the systems go down when you're out in rural Africa, so I'm not alarmed yet. Let me have a search and check that everything's okay out there. I'll get back to you."

"Thanks, Kyra. That'll put me at ease, knowing you're on the case."

Kyra opened up her laptop and looked on a site only available to her as a journalist. It gave all the latest news, right up to the minute, so in some cases news hadn't even hit the main outlets yet. She found a small insignificant report of some fighting having broken out in Ethiopia, and on further searching found that it was on the Ethiopian side of the Sudanese border. She knew from previous experience that with any uprisings, however serious, the police would put out a curfew and it would be hard for Lukas and Nils to travel back to Addis. If anything had happened, she was sure Lukas' father would know.

Kyra gave him a ring, but he hadn't heard anything. He said he'd contact Mahmoud, his man in Addis, to find out the latest.

"I shouldn't worry too much," he said. "If Mahmoud has sent them with someone local, then I'm sure they'll be well looked after. As long as they stay out of the way of any police or militia, they'll be fine."

"Thank you, James. I'll wait to hear from you."

Kyra pondered whether or not to tell Jess, but thought in the long run it would be better to keep her up to date. When she spoke to her, she played down the situation, saying most likely the locals were shutting the roads down for a while to keep control, and that James was on the case to find out what he could.

"Do you want me to come over, or would you like to come over here," Kyra said. "We can have a meal together. I'll take you out to downtown Didsbury." She laughed.

"Thanks. That'd be great," Jess said. "I know I'll agonise over every second I don't hear from him if I sit here on my own. What time do you want me?"

After they'd arranged a time, Kyra finished off her writing then double-checked to see if there were any updates on the situation in Ethiopia. There was nothing new.

Jess arrived in the early evening and almost threw herself into Kyra's arms.

"I'm sorry, but I'm so worried. Lukas always rings me when he's away and not to have heard from him for over twenty-four hours just doesn't feel right."

Kyra led the way into her kitchen, where she poured Jess a large gin.

"Listen, I know this sounds like an excuse, but believe me, I know from working with journalists who are in countries where fighting breaks out, that the local police lock everything down, and unless you're in a major city, you don't stand a cat in hell's chance of getting any information out. Come on, have a drink and please try to relax."

Jess took a large sip, but to Kyra she still looked incredibly stressed.

"Places like Ethiopia often have local skirmishes that break out. To us it seems like something quite dramatic, but to them it's an almost monthly occurrence, so I bet they'll be in touch very soon."

Taking a drink of her own gin, she sat opposite Jess, who had plonked herself down on one of the chairs around the small kitchen island.

"I've booked us a table at a local place I love, so once we've finished this, we'll make our way over there and have a few more before we eat. That sound okay?"

"Yes. Thanks, Kyra. I know I'm probably over-reacting, but as I said, I'm not used to Lukas being away without contact. I'm sure you're right. You know far more than me about this sort of thing."

Kyra noticed that Jess' smile seemed a little forced, though far more relaxed than when she'd arrived.

"Has James been in touch with you?" she asked Jess.

"Yes. He said he'd contacted Mahmoud, but he hadn't heard from them either, but he told James what you've just mentioned, about local police taking over. He told me not to fret about it too, however I'm not convinced that he isn't worried, either."

"Let's enjoy our meal, try to push it out of our minds. If you want, you can stay tonight, and then drive home tomorrow morning. You'll be able to have a few more drinks than you would if you go back tonight."

Jess looked relieved. "Thank you, that'd be great."

Kyra took Jess to a different restaurant to where she'd taken Nils, but one that she and Fran particularly liked, called *Cherrish.* On her visit she'd asked the owner why that name. Matt had told her he loved cherries so he decided to create a pun on his favourite fruit that he *cherished,* opting for the double 'r' in his business name. His particular expertise lay in creating the most amazing vegetarian dishes that were incredibly flavoursome; even the most carnivorous of Kyra's friends had never once complained about not getting any meat.

During the meal, Jess and Kyra's conversation turned to the guys.

"Things seem to be going well with you and Nils. Are you considering moving in together?"

Kyra smiled. "Not really, no. We both like our own space and I think we've both lived alone for too long, so I think we're comfortable with moving between Manchester and Stockholm for the time being."

"What if you have children? Won't that make things difficult?" Jess asked.

Surprised that Jess had gone down that route of thinking, Kyra considered her answer. "No, not really. We've never discussed children. I'm not that keen on having any and I don't think Nils is, to be honest."

Jess looked shocked. "Don't you want his babies?"

Kyra nearly choked on her mouthful of food. "Erm, should I? Do you think I love him less by not wanting his babies?" Kyra could see that this had thrown Jess. "Why do you think it's okay to expect me to want his babies?"

"I'm sorry, Kyra. I didn't mean to be so intrusive. It's just that, I want to have Lukas' babies – that is, if he wants me to have them. But, I can't imagine being with someone I love and not wanting their babies."

“There’s nothing wrong with wanting children, but there’s also nothing wrong with not wanting them. Nils and I both love our careers, and if we had children, I’d want to give up my career to look after them. Call me selfish if you like, but I’d rather not have any, continue my career, and be with the man I love. We have the choice these days, and besides there are far too many unwanted children in the world already.” Kyra returned to eating her meal, feeling a little surprised by Jess’ questions. Because Jess was that much younger than her, she’d always thought of her as being more progressive in her outlook. She’d obviously been wrong.

Jess focused on eating her meal and had gone very quiet. Kyra wondered if she felt awkward.

“I’ll tell you what, you have them for me and we can enjoy your children with you – if you want us to.” Kyra smiled at her.

“That’d be great. If Lukas ever asks me to marry him, I know he’d want you two to be involved in our family.”

“Have you talked about children then?” Kyra asked.

“Not really, but his cousin Greta had a baby last year, Felix – he’s so cute. Lukas loves being an uncle. You should see him with the baby.”

They continued their meal, far more relaxed, and after a few more drinks, Jess and Kyra were giggling about the inanest things.

When they got back to Kyra’s, they were both ready to sleep. Full of food and both rather tipsy.

While they were eating breakfast the next morning, Kyra’s phone rang. It was James.

“I tried to ring Jess last night. Do you know where she is?” he asked.

“She’s here with me. Do you have any news?”

Jess looked up from her breakfast, a worried expression on her face.

Kyra mouthed at her. "It's all good."

"Yes, Mahmoud contacted me. It's as I thought. They're stuck in Gedo, and the local police have banned any movement around the area. As soon as things get back to normal, Mahmoud promised to let me know."

"Thanks, James. Do you want to speak to Jess?"

Kyra passed her phone over to Jess so she could speak to Lukas' father.

While they were talking, Kyra made more coffee, and Jess looked far calmer after her conversation with James.

"What did I tell you – things will sort themselves out. We just have to wait patiently until the local police open the roads up again." Kyra handed a mug of coffee over to Jess.

What Jess didn't need to know was that, even though the roads were closed and the police had set a curfew, it didn't mean that as white Europeans they were one hundred percent safe. Kyra prayed that the man Mahmoud had sent with Nils and Lukas knew how to keep them out of danger.

24
SEPTEMBER 2023
MANCHESTER

Lukas had spoken to his dad. After hearing about their find, he'd hired a private jet to collect them from Addis Ababa, due to the special cargo they were carrying. With Mahmoud's help, he'd also arranged for someone to seal the bone in a hermetic container before it left Ethiopia. When Lukas' and Nils' plane landed at Manchester, the company commissioned to run extremely expensive DNA tests would collect the bone and deliver it securely to their labs.

Jess and Kyra weren't told any of this. They were under the impression that it was because of the ordeal out in Gedo that Lukas and Nils were flown home by private jet.

In the VIP aviation centre at Manchester airport, Jess and Kyra were drinking G&Ts when Lukas and Nils walked in.

"Calming your nerves?" Lukas asked.

Jess burst into tears, whereas Kyra remained calmer, but she hugged Nils as if she'd never let him go.

"I think I'll have to go away more often," he whispered in between kisses.

Finally settled in the lounge bar with drinks all round, Lukas and Nils explained how they'd managed to get out of the country. Lukas was bursting with their news. He couldn't wait to tell the girls what they'd found – which they'd agreed to keep secret until now.

Unable to contain himself any longer, Lukas began. "We've got some news—"

"So have I," Kyra said. "Did you know Cole has an identical twin?"

With some evident disappointment, Nils said, "That was our news."

"But, we can top that," Lukas said. "We have something that may well be able to prove that Cole isn't Cole."

"This isn't a competition, Lukas," Jess said.

"I know. It's my friend we're talking about. I'm not exactly thrilled about this, but the truth must come out."

Kyra nodded. "You do realise Sofia must know who she's living with. She went to school with them both," she said. "Well, I spoke to a guy who went to school with all three of them, and interestingly he thought that Sofia was keen on Caleb back then, but he's not sure if they ever got together."

Lukas answered. "I agree. I believe she must know who she's living with, too. That's what's so odd. We managed to find the guy who arrived just after the accident happened. Megasu – that's his name – told us that his mate Sam looked just like the dead guy. And Sam told Megasu to hide the body and give all the dead man's papers to him. So, we can only presume that Sam is, in fact, Caleb, Cole's twin."

Kyra and Jess looked at each other. "Shit, that's a harsh thing to do to your brother, even if he is dead," said Kyra.

"And," said Nils, "I found a human bone under a rock near the accident site, where Megasu had hidden the body. That's why we flew in on private jet. Lukas' dad has arranged for the bone to be tested for DNA."

Jess looked thoughtful. "But why would Sofia live with him, if he isn't her husband? I don't get that. Surely, she wouldn't welcome him into her bed after he's changed places with her dead husband. I mean, look how loved-up they've been. It doesn't make sense."

They all agreed they needed to confront 'Cole' to see if he was, as they suspected, Caleb.

A couple of nights later, when everyone returned to their respective homes in Manchester, Lukas phoned 'Cole' to invite him out for a drink with him and Nils.

The three of them met up in a busy, noisy pub where, should they end up arguing, no one would notice. Nils and Lukas were already sitting at a table in a corner when 'Cole' walked in.

Lukas leapt to his feet to greet him. "What can I get you, mate – your usual?"

"Yes, thanks."

Lukas went to the bar to get the drinks, leaving Nils to chat to 'Cole'.

As Lukas returned with the drinks, 'Cole' asked, "Sofia tells me you guys have been out to Ethiopia. What were you doing out there?"

Lukas answered. "We wanted to see the accident site, to see if there was anything missed that could lead to the cause of the crash."

"Why would you do that?"

"Well, it all seems a little weird," Lukas said.

“What do you mean, weird? I had a near-fatal accident and you want to go and visit. That’s taking rubber-necking to a new level. Now, that’s weird.”

Nils looked confused by the odd term, so Lukas quickly explained then took a deep breath before getting the conversation back on track.

“I don’t think you are who you are pretending to be,” Lukas said. He noticed a minute change in ‘Cole’s’ expression, which disappeared as quickly as it had appeared.

“C’mon, mate, who do you think I am?”

“I think you’re Caleb, and your twin brother, Cole, actually died in the accident.” Lukas took a large gulp of his beer.

Again, he caught a flicker of something in ‘Cole’s’ eyes, and wondered if it was surprise at their knowledge about him being a twin.

“You’re not saying anything, Nils. Are you going along with this twisted insinuation of my so-called best friend?”

“I’m just here to support Lukas, watch and listen.”

“Well, I don’t know what you think you’ve found, but no, I’m not Caleb. He’s dead. He committed suicide when he left prison,” ‘Cole’ replied.

“Actually, Caleb’s body was never found and the police only have him down as ‘presumed dead’. So, I think you needed your brother’s identity for some reason, and when he died in that accident, you took advantage of the macabre situation. And you’ve been impersonating him since you got back.” Lukas glared at ‘Cole’.

‘Cole’ finished off the beer he’d been drinking, and still keeping his cool, stood to leave.

“Well, good luck proving I’m not Cole, mate! Identical twins have identical DNA.”

With that, he stormed out of the pub.

Lukas, his hand shaking, picked up his beer for a well-needed drink. “He obviously hasn’t heard about the new DNA tests.” He smiled.

Nils looked around surreptitiously, and using a clean tissue rather than his hand, picked up and then slipped Cole’s glass into a plastic bag, putting both into his backpack.

“Well, in a few weeks, we’ll know for sure,” Nils said. “I’ll get this sent to the lab, along with the comb Mahmoud gave us from Cole’s belongings he left behind in Addis. We’re lucky your dad has the money to pay for the test, because it’s still relatively new and usually too costly for most police forces to even bother. I’ve only read about a few forces in the world making use of the test. The cost would certainly be an issue here, because we have no strong evidence to prove anything either way. The outcome of this test will, hopefully, be our proof.”

A few days later, Lukas, Kyra and Nils visited the police station to talk to Detective Liam Reeves, who Kyra had worked with before. He told them exactly what they’d presumed – that without any real proof, he could not start an investigation. However, if the DNA test came back proving that Cole was actually his twin brother, Caleb, then they could bring him in for questioning.

25

SEPTEMBER 2023

LIVERPOOL

With a large glass of gin on the table in front of her, Susie sat in the same corner of the pub where she'd met Lenny several weeks ago, the same time she'd last seen Kev. She was surprised to see him again so soon.

"Hi, how are you doing, love?" Kev said. He nodded towards the man with him. "This is a mate of mine, Marius. Can we join you, Susie?"

Susie signalled her agreement, and before sitting, Marius stretched over the table and shook her hand.

"Very pleased to meet you."

"You too, love. That's not a Liverpudlian accent. Where are you from, Marius?"

"Holland. I'm just over for a few days to visit Kev."

"Ooh, that's nice. You've got some fancy friends, Kev."

Kev laughed nervously and gave Marius a furtive glance before continuing. "Susie, can you tell Marius what you told me about Caleb Drake? You remember, when that journalist asked you for information?"

"Okay. Ooh, look my gin's going down fast." She looked at Kev hopefully. Taking the hint, he disappeared off to the bar.

Marius asked, “Do you know why the journalist wanted to know about Caleb Drake?”

“Yes, sort of – well not completely. When I showed him that Caleb was missing, presumed dead, he seemed to think that it wasn’t what the person he worked for wanted to hear. I think there was some question about identity.”

“What else did he talk about?”

“He told me about Tony dying in prison. I went to school with him, you know. Ooh, thanks, Kev—” She interrupted her answer to finish off the gin left in her previous glass before beginning the one Kev had just put in front of her. “Then, Kev asked me about this Drake fella. Why is he so important?”

Kev answered, “Well, we hadn’t heard he’d died, and we’re not sure if he is actually dead. Another friend of ours, who hasn’t seen Drake for years, wants to get back in touch with him. He was surprised to hear that he’d died. Like us, he’s not convinced. Do you think you could find anything else about Drake or his family? We can always ask them where he is.”

Marius added very quickly, “We can make it worth your while.” He pushed some notes over to her. “There’s plenty more where that came from, if you do find any more information.”

“Ooh, thank you. I’ll see what I can do.”

Kev slid a note over to her with his phone number. “Ring me as soon as you find anything.”

He bent down and kissed her on the cheek and he and Marius left.

A couple of weeks later, Kev received a call from Susie. He went to the pub to meet her, this time alone, as Marius had returned to Holland, seemingly happy in the knowledge that Kev had things under control.

"What have you got for me?" he asked, placing a large gin in front of her.

"Thanks, love." She took a sip. "Kev, what's so important about the Drakes? I'm not getting anyone into trouble, am I? I mean, I didn't like to ask when your mate was here, but why is Marius so keen to give me money to search?"

"No, you're not going to get in trouble. We just want to know if our mate is still alive or not. You know what it's like. People have problems, disappear for a bit, and then reappear – well, our friend wants to know if his mate, Caleb, is still alive. Marius is just showing his gratitude that you've tried to find out for us. This other friend who's looking for Caleb means a lot to him." He gave Susie a broad smile, hoping she'd accept his answer. "So, what have you found out?"

"Well, there's been some chatter around the nick. It seems someone visited Detective Reeves to talk about the suspicion of false identity, and guess the name I heard being talked about?"

"Go on, enlighten me."

"Cole Drake."

"Isn't that Caleb's twin brother?" Kev asked.

"How do you know that?" Susie asked.

"Don't worry yourself about that, but I just do. So, what did you hear?"

"So, I heard these two guys talking over a cigarette – of course, they didn't know anyone was listening. One said, 'I wonder if she knows. I mean, would you be able to tell the difference if they're twins?' Then the other said, 'I don't think I'd care. I mean, I would, if she was my brother's wife, wouldn't you? She's got a great arse. Talk about keeping it in the family.'

"Then they'd both burst out laughing. When they mentioned twins, my ears pricked up. So, I asked one of the other secretaries about it and she was like, 'Don't tell anyone, but someone has been in to talk to the detectives because they think one twin has died and the other is living as him.' How bizarre is that?"

Kev's mind raced through a whole load of scenarios. He hadn't expected this much information, and he knew Marius would be interested to hear the news.

"Susie, you are incredible. Thank you. Here's the money Marius promised you."

He pushed an envelope that looked fit to bursting across the table to her.

As she pulled it towards herself and carefully opened it, Kev got up to leave.

By the time he'd reached the door, Susie had closed the envelope and was guarding its precious contents with her arm.

Once outside, Kev reached into his pocket for his mobile phone and swiped through his contacts to call Marius.

"Marius, I think Caleb Drake might still be alive. What do you want us to do?"

"Start following him and maybe you'll find out which twin he is. If it is Caleb, we'll get the bastard."

26

SEPTEMBER 2023
MANCHESTER

Caleb hadn't seemed the same since the night when he'd met up with Lukas and Nils. Sofia tried to find out what had happened, but each time she asked about it, he got annoyed and told her to stop nagging. Easier said than done! Caleb wasn't as relaxed as he'd been after he'd first come out of hospital, a time she now thought of as their 'honeymoon' period. Now he seemed far more stressed, and although their love life continued to be amazing, he frequently lost his temper with her.

A few days earlier, Sofia thought she'd noticed someone staring at her when she'd been in town shopping, and she'd noticed him several times. When she'd mentioned it to Caleb, he'd told her not to be silly and to stop being paranoid. However, another night as they'd left to go out for a meal, it had been him that had kept turning around as if he was looking for someone.

"What's the matter, babe? Do you think I'm right? Is someone following us?" she'd said.

He'd instantly snapped at her. "Don't be stupid. Who'd be following us?" He'd put his arm around her and had encouraged her to walk quicker.

Unusually, during the meal, their conversation had seemed stilted and Sofia couldn't wait to get back to their apartment.

Later, when they'd been in bed, Caleb had leant over to kiss her and pull her towards him, but she'd pushed him off.

"Caleb, do you think it's those men you told me about and they know you're not Cole?"

He'd answered too quickly. "No, how would they know I'm not Cole? I've told you, you're just panicking." He'd pulled her towards him again, this time with far more force. They'd made love, but due to his mood, it was with a roughness she hadn't experienced before, and Sofia had felt uncomfortable and a little scared.

On another day, Caleb's phone had rung several times. She'd seen him answer, but each time, there'd been no conversation. "Who's ringing you, babe?" she'd asked.

"No one important."

And now, several days later, they'd just received a delivery of a beautiful box filled with flowers, Sofia presumed. However, when she went to open it, she found the box full of dead, blackened roses. There was a card, too, and it read: *'Sorry to hear of your loss.'*

Sofia screamed and dropped the card on the floor.

Caleb rushed into the room and grabbed her into his arms. "Sofe, you're okay. I'm here."

Sofia clung to him for some time, shaken by the horrible 'gift' and terrified by the wording on the card.

When she'd calmed down, she said, "We need to tell the police, Caleb. I can't cope with being scared all the time."

"We can't. We're stuck. If it's who I think it is, then they obviously have a suspicion that I'm not Cole. They're certainly not going to go to the police about me, but it's all getting complicated. Lukas doesn't believe I'm who I say I am, and if he's spoken to the police, then they'll be suspicious of me already. Yes, I've been impersonating Cole, and even though I didn't kill him, pretending to be him is a crime. I don't want to go back to jail, Sofe."

Sofia kissed him. "No, I don't want you to go back either, but I'm scared. Do you think they really know something, or they're just trying to find out? Either way, I can't cope, thinking they're out there waiting for an opportunity to kill you."

Caleb told Sofia to sit down. "The police may already know something is going on," he said.

He told her what had happened on the night he'd met Lukas and Nils. That they'd confronted him about his identity and told him they were going to speak to the police.

"They tried a bluff, telling me they had found one of Cole's bones and they're going to check for DNA. I told them they were wasting their time – as identical twins, we have identical DNA. How are they going to prove it?"

Slightly shell-shocked by this revelation, Sofia watched as Caleb went to pour them both a strong drink.

Sitting down next to her, he continued, "I really don't want to get the police involved. Once they start questioning you, they somehow change the meaning of your words, manage to turn everything upside down, and before you know it you're giving things away. No, we'll keep a good look out to see if someone actually is following us, okay?"

Sofia nodded, though she wasn't convinced.

After that, every time they went out, it became more obvious that Caleb was checking to see if they were being followed. When they were on foot, he told Sofia he hadn't noticed anyone. However, on one occasion when they drove to the hospital for

Caleb's medication, Sofia noticed he'd taken a very odd route home. When they got back to the apartment, she asked him why he'd taken the long way around.

"I think I noticed a black car following us. I saw it a few times. That's why I changed the route – I tried to get ahead far enough so I'd lose them."

"Did you?"

"Yes, but surely they know where we live. It must have been them that sent the flowers. I think they want me to know they're following us."

"Caleb, I can't lose you. I don't want to be a widow twice."

He kissed her and they stood holding on to each other in silent comfort.

That night, neither of them slept well. Caleb was tossing and turning, and Sofia kept waking and lay listening for any unusual sounds. She envisaged all types of scenarios where someone might try to break in to kill them. However, she calmed down by reminding herself that it would be hard for a stranger to get access to the inside of the apartment. Although the area they lived in was considered to be safe, Manchester, like any other large city, had its fair share of gangs and crime. The ground floor had plenty of security cameras around, which is one of the main reasons Cole had chosen this particular building.

By the time she woke in the morning, Caleb was already up and dressed. He brought her some coffee and sat on the edge of the bed.

"Sofe, I've been thinking. We need to leave. I'm certain that what's left of the Johnson gang know that I'm here and that I'm not Cole. I think we'd be better off making a run for it."

Sofia nearly spat her coffee out.

"What? No, I don't want to move. We've got to go to the police. This is silly. Impersonating your brother can't be that big of a crime, surely? Please, let's just talk to the police. You haven't done anything wrong. You've served your time."

"I don't trust them enough. I'm sorry, but no. Please, Sofe, come with me. We can go abroad. I know lots of great places in Spain where we could live a great life. The weather is better than here, sunny and healthier. So much better than dismal Manchester."

Sofia glared at him. "Why should we give up our life and move? Sunny weather isn't everything."

Caleb looked deep into her eyes and said, "Because I want to live, so I can carry on loving you."

27

Sofia could hear Caleb banging around in the bedroom, and went in to investigate. Standing in the doorway, she couldn't believe the sight in front of her. Caleb chucked clothes into a large bag sat on the bed.

"What are you doing?"

Caleb stopped mid-throw, holding a pair of rolled-up jeans in his hand. "I'm sorry, but I can't stay any longer. Please, Sofe, come with me. I don't want to live without you again. Now we've had time together, I can't imagine being without you. But if I stay here, we could both end up dead, and I know for certain, I will."

"Caleb, if you really cared so much, you'd go to the police. I don't understand why you won't."

"I've already told you, I don't trust them. How do you think the Johnsons know I'm still alive?"

Sofia shrugged.

"Because someone somewhere, maybe a police informer, has passed on information to them. I don't know for sure, but how else can they have found out? What I do know is, they're vicious. They won't stop until I'm dead."

Sofia started crying. "But, if they're watching us, they'll see us leaving, surely?"

"Sofe, why have you stood by me these past months?"

"Because I love you."

"So, isn't that enough?"

Sofia stared at him. "Isn't it enough? I've lied for you." Her voice grew louder with each word. "I've accepted everything you've told me. I believed you when you said you didn't kill Cole. But, I honestly don't think running is going to help. They'll just come looking for us wherever we are." She wiped the tears off her cheeks and then rubbed together her mascara-stained fingers. "I honestly believe we need to face up to this and go to the police. I don't want to spend my life on the run. No matter how much I love you. I'm sorry. No, I'm not leaving."

Caleb dropped the jeans he was holding and walked over to Sofia. Putting his hands on her shoulders, he looked directly into her face and said, "I'm sorry, too, but you either trust me and come with me, or you stay here." Then he turned back and continued to pack.

Sofia walked out of the room, slamming the door behind her.

Half an hour later, Caleb walked into the lounge, carrying his bag, wearing a baseball hat pulled low over his eyes and the collar of his jacket pulled up around his neck.

"Do you really think that's a good enough disguise?" she asked him.

"It'll have to do. I can go out of the maintenance exit and hope nobody is watching there."

"Are they likely to be that stupid?"

"Maybe. Hopefully. Anyway, I don't think they'll come after you. Tony Johnson promised that it was only me he'd come after, but I suppose now he's dead, it depends on who's left."

Caleb leant in and kissed her before quickly rushing out of the door.

She sank onto the sofa, and she let silent tears stream down her face as a feeling of dread rose from deep within her stomach. *What have I done?*

Sofia didn't know how long she'd sat motionless on the sofa, but she noticed that it had grown darker. Slowly, she got up and switched the lamps on around the room before sitting back down on the sofa again. The apartment felt empty without Caleb.

She jumped when there was a loud knock on the door. *Caleb's come back.* Without pausing to think, she went to let him in.

Standing there were two men wearing balaclavas.

Sofia gasped as they rushed inside. Before she could even scream, one of them pushed her back into the room. Then as he moved forward to grab her, he knocked over one of the kitchen stools.

Once he'd captured her, he put his hand over her mouth, holding her tightly. She was unable to move; no match for a man of his stature.

"You're going to keep quiet and walk out of here with us without giving us any problems. We're parked in the underground parking, so we're not going to bump into anyone who can help. Got it?"

He pulled a small gun from his pocket and waved it in her direction.

Sofia nodded vigorously. Despite being scared, she still wondered how they'd managed to get access to the underground parking.

The other man took a roll of tape from his pocket and taped her hands behind her.

"We're not going to gag you, if you promise to keep quiet, but one sound and you'll regret it."

She nodded again, glancing at his gun. There was only one other apartment on their floor. She knew the couple were away, so these guys would be able to get her in the lift easily, without any witnesses. But then she remembered the cameras. How would they get past those?

As they took her out of the apartment, one man in front of her, the other holding on to her and pushing her from behind, she saw that the cameras had been tilted into an upwards angle towards the ceiling.

When they got to their car, they did tie a gag over her mouth, and they put a cotton bag over her head before making her lie down on the backseat.

Keeping quiet wasn't difficult at all. Her fear meant she could barely breathe. Caleb had told her she would be safe – they wouldn't come after her. Why had she been so stubborn? Sick with fear, she whispered, "Caleb, why didn't I go with you?"

Sofia had no idea where they were taking her. She could hear the noise of traffic, the sounds of the night; when the car stopped at lights, people's voices; somewhere in the distance, a train clattering over tracks; and then eventually after the sound of traffic had eased, the sound of something metallic. She instantly recognised it as a sound similar to a garage door.

The car stopped and the two men unceremoniously pulled her from the backseat, dragging her across a large space before forcing her to sit on a chair. She still wore the bag over her head, and they taped her feet to the chair legs then ran tape around her body too. Sofia tried to squirm away from the hands of one of the men who gratuitously groped her breasts as he bound her body.

After they'd finished, they left her sitting enclosed in darkness before walking away.

Her fear strengthened as her mind worked overtime, wondering if they were going to leave her there to die.

After what felt like ages, she heard men's voices and then their footsteps as someone approached her and pulled the bag from her head.

Sofia blinked and looked up to see three men this time, all wearing balaclavas, standing in front of her.

"You're going to send a message to your boyfriend. You're going to tell him that he needs to turn himself over to us, and we'll let you go without harming you – as long as he doesn't go to the police or do anything stupid. Have you got that?"

Sofia nodded. One of the three men walked over to her.

"Don't waste your breath screaming when I remove your gag. No one can hear you."

He removed her gag, and she desperately held back the urge to scream, instead gratefully breathing in several mouthfuls of air.

The man moved away from her. Using her own phone, which they'd taken from her, he started to film.

"Go on. Tell Caleb what I told you to say."

Sofia did as she'd been directed. Between sobs, which she couldn't control, she relayed their message to Caleb.

As soon as they'd finished, she watched the one with her phone send the video over to Caleb.

The three men left the room, taking her phone with them. Sofia was alone in the large, dark, cold, empty warehouse. She looked around at the gloomy surroundings, her heart sinking. She began to think she might actually die after all. *What if Caleb doesn't come for me?* Surprised then ashamed as water trickled down her legs, she realised she'd wet herself. Her tears began to fall freely as she wailed uncontrollably, completely terrified and humiliated. *Please, Caleb. I need you.*

By the time two of the men returned, Sofia had closed down and stared vacantly into the blackness. She had no idea of time, so it could have been minutes or even hours since they'd left. Still surrounded by darkness and with no idea of where she was, her body had become stiff from remaining still for so long. She vaguely felt some awareness as they cut the tape that bound her feet and body then dragged her over to a pile of sacks, where they lay her, none too gently. They taped her feet and hands back together and left her.

It took some time for her to notice that they'd gone. She cried out for Caleb. *Does he love me enough?* she wondered. Would he come back? She prayed to the God she'd renounced many years ago that he would.

28

Caleb walked back into the apartment around midnight. He'd almost got all the way to the airport before his conscience got the better of him. He knew he couldn't exist without Sofia. Not this time.

Looking around the apartment, he was surprised to see the lamps were on around the room and also to find one of the kitchen stools on its side. After dumping his bag on the floor, he returned the stool to its normal position, with an unsettling feeling that something was wrong.

Although they usually stayed up late, he thought Sofe might have gone to bed early, so he walked over to the bedroom where he hoped to find her sleeping. As soon as he saw the empty bed, he pulled his phone out of his pocket to ring Jess, the only person who he could imagine Sofia might have turned to.

His phone battery was dead. Annoyed, he managed to find Sofia's charger and he plugged his phone in.

After waiting a few minutes for enough charge to turn it on, he heard his phone ping. He saw a message from Sofia and felt relieved, until he saw what the message contained.

"Christ no! Sofia."

Watching the video, he became angrier and angrier. When the video finished, a second message came through from someone he hadn't seen for years. Kev, one of Tony Johnson's right-hand men. He always assumed that he'd be in prison with the rest of the gang.

"I hope you're watching this, Drake. If you don't turn yourself in, in the next couple of hours, we'll kill her. We don't want to, but we will. If you turn yourself in, then we'll let her go, and that'll be it. Your life for hers. So far, she hasn't seen us, so for her sake, don't take long to get back to us."

Caleb stared at the phone.

"You bastard!" he said into the stillness of the apartment. "You absolute fucking bastard."

He rang Sofia's phone back.

Kev answered. "Drake, you going to be a good boy then, and come and get your girl?"

As much as he tried, he was unable to contain his anger, and he shouted a string of expletives down the phone.

"Calm down, Drake. That isn't going to endear you to me, now, is it? Especially as my opinion of you is pretty low to start with."

Caleb took a deep breath. "I'll turn myself over to you, but you have to promise that you don't let Sofia see your faces. I want assurances that if I get a friend to drive me over, you give Sofia to me, and once I've seen them drive away safely, I'm all yours."

"And how do we know you won't have police in the car, or have them hiding down the way somewhere?"

"Because I value Sofia's life more than my own. I will bring a woman with me who will drive, but you have to promise you'll let them get completely clear before you take me."

"You're convincing, Drake. I think I believe you. But, if we see anything suspicious that looks like police, or armed police, we'll kill her and you on the spot. You listening?"

"Yes, I'm won't be doing anything stupid to jeopardise Sofia's life. You have my word."

"Mm, and we all know how good the word of a rat is, don't we?" Kev abruptly ended the call.

Aware how stressed he'd become, Caleb relaxed his shoulders and breathed out. He poured himself a large whisky and sat on the sofa.

Caleb didn't want to leave Sofia with Kev and his guys for long, but he knew they wouldn't agree to the exchange taking place in daylight hours. That also meant, though, he would have a little longer to persuade someone to go with him to get Sofia. And the person he wanted to go with him was Kyra. He didn't know why, but he trusted her the most.

He leant back on the sofa, feeling completely defeated. *Sofe, why didn't you just come with me? We could have got away free and lived a happy life far away from here.*

Caleb sat completely still for a long time. Part of him wanted to grab his bag and run, but for the first time in his life, something nagged deep inside his gut.

But he had to leave. He had no choice.

Having decided, he stood, but he only managed a few steps, when without any warning, he began to silently weep, unable to stop. He couldn't leave her. He'd always loved Sofia. She'd taken him back; she'd lied for him – despite all the knowledge he'd shared with her. She'd accepted everything he'd told her. Her love for him was immeasurable. He knew he couldn't walk away. Not this time. He had to put someone else first – before himself.

He sat back down on the sofa, and letting free his emotions for the first time as an adult man, he cried himself to sleep.

Caleb woke as the bright daylight streamed into the apartment. As the memory of the night before kicked in, he was suddenly wide awake and restless. He found Kyra's number on his phone, and although it was still pretty early, he didn't care.

"Kyra, it's me."

She sounded surprised.

"I need your help, but I need you to keep this between you and me. Please don't tell Nils, and definitely don't tell Lukas – not even where you're going. Can you come over to our apartment?"

"Er, yes. It's a bit early. Is everything okay?"

"Not really, but I can't explain over the phone. Please can you make it as quick as you can?"

"Okay. Nils is still sleeping, so I'll leave him a note, saying that some urgent work turned up. He'll understand that. I've got to get dressed, so see you in a while."

Kyra arrived about an hour later. After inviting her in and asking her to sit down, Caleb made them both coffee and then joined her on the sofa.

"Where's Sofia?"

"That's what I need to talk to you about."

He explained what had happened, and confirmed that she, Lukas and Nils were right, and he was Caleb, not Cole. Then he explained about the Johnsons finding him and the fact he thought there must be someone inside the police. He left the most important and dramatic event to last – that Sofia had been kidnapped.

"My God, Caleb, I'm sorry. I think I'm partly to blame for that. I asked a mate in Liverpool to find out about Cole's background, because he'd actually never shared much with Lukas. I mean, we didn't know you were twins until after I'd spoken to my mate. Then Lukas and Nils corroborated that, during their time in Africa. And you're right about the Johnsons having someone inside the police. There's an informant, in Liverpool."

At that moment Caleb nearly lost it. His hands clenched as he wanted to slap Kyra for interfering in their lives, but he stopped himself because he knew he had to get her on his side.

Even though Caleb hadn't been in touch with Cole since he'd left Liverpool – they hadn't even spoken – it was hard. As identical twins, there always seemed to be an invisible link between them. In this moment, he realised he hadn't actually grieved Cole's death. But now he might lose Sofia, too. Fear and grief filled his entire being and hit him hard. For once, it gave him an insight into how Lukas must have felt losing Cole. His brother.

Kyra interrupted his thoughts by asking, "You didn't kill Cole, did you?"

"No, I didn't. I just took advantage of a horrible accident, and you can blame me for that all you like."

Kyra stayed quiet then asked, "So, why call me now instead of going to the police?"

"Because the people that have Sofia want me to turn myself over to them in exchange for her."

"And you don't think the police could sort it out better than you?"

"No, not with this gang. It's the only way I'm going to get Sofia back alive."

Kyra tried several times to persuade Caleb that they'd be better off contacting the police, but he wouldn't even consider it. He assured her that he'd do everything to keep her safe. That they would park the car at a distance so that as soon as Sofia was free they could safely drive away, and he'd hand himself over.

"I'm not happy about that idea, Caleb. Please consider talking to the police. We could have them waiting somewhere nearby so that they don't spook the Johnsons?"

"Definitely not. They'll know if anything or anyone moves

who shouldn't. That's why they've been so successful for years. I can't chance putting Sofe's life in danger. Please, do it my way. If there's any way I can escape, then once you have her, I will, but her safety is everything."

Kyra agreed to Caleb's plan, but with some reticence. She wondered if she dare get in touch with her contact at the station, but then if anything went wrong – she didn't know what Caleb would do. And she didn't want Sofia's death on her hands.

Caleb asked Kyra to stay with him and said he'd contact the gang and arrange the time for the exchange.

At one point, Kyra's mobile rang, but she let it go to messages. "It's not a problem. Nils will think I'm working," she said.

Caleb ordered them a pizza to eat as they waited. But she couldn't eat, and neither, it seemed, could he.

29

Caleb occasionally glanced at Kyra as she drove them to the exchange point at the old docks. No words passed between them. What was there to talk about? Caleb had made his choice, and he'd persuaded Kyra to help him. There was no going back.

She impressed him, though, with how calm she appeared. She didn't seem to be nervous at all and gave the impression of someone completely focused on her driving and the task ahead, however she may have been feeling on the inside.

As they drove towards the warehouse, Caleb made a point of emphasising where the exits were, which would be the escape route for her and Sofia. The whole area looked rundown, apart from a few very small units where work vans and lorries were parked up. Depressingly desolate, where people were trying to make a living from nothing.

They eventually stopped at the entrance to a large warehouse site. The look of the site brought back memories for Caleb of the warehouse where the bungled heist had taken place and his subsequent arrest. The thought flashed across his mind that maybe this was a sick joke by Kev, until he realised his own memory was playing tricks. That warehouse had been in Liverpool. *I must keep a clear head – keep my emotions in check.*

Kyra turned the car around so it faced away from the building ready for their getaway.

"You stay in the car. Whatever happens, don't get out for any reason, and if I tell you to leave, you go without us."

"Hopefully it won't come to that."

"Hopefully not. I'll bring Sofia to you, okay?"

Kyra nodded. "You don't have to do this, Caleb."

"Yes, I do. She's the only woman I've ever loved, and I need her to be safe. Tell her that, please. Take care of her – promise me." Again, Kyra nodded.

Caleb walked towards the warehouse, cautiously looking around as he did so. He was checking for any sign of men hidden in the undergrowth, but he couldn't see anyone. Just maybe they'd keep to their side of the bargain. As he got closer, he stopped and took a sharp intake of breath as he saw two men holding on to Sofia. She hunched slightly forward, her eyes blindfolded, and by the angle of her arms, he presumed her hands were taped behind her back.

The men, who all wore balaclavas, were having to hold Sofia upright. Despite the balaclavas, Caleb instantly knew who the men were, by their size and the way they moved.

"Stay where you are," one of them ordered.

Caleb stopped and waited while they walked towards him. He knew they'd stopped within viewing distance of the car, where Kyra sat with the engine running.

"You lead her to the car and come straight back once she's inside."

Caleb reached out for Sofia's arms. Seeing her visibly broken, a searing pain took his breath away. Though as far as he could see, she wasn't physically hurt. She could barely stand, and struggling to keep calm, she visibly shook – whether due to the cold, fear or both.

He pulled her towards him and whispered in her ear. "You're safe now, Sofe. Come on."

"Caleb," she whimpered. "Caleb, you came."

Slowly, holding on to her tightly, he started to walk her towards the car, away from the men.

"Of course I came. How could I leave you, when you're the love of my life?"

Sofia stumbled, falling over her own feet. "Please, take the blindfold off. I can't see where I'm going."

"I can't. You mustn't see them. Trust me. I'm going to get you out of here."

They eventually reached the car, and he opened the passenger door. He took a knife from his pocket and cut the tape holding her wrists together, before helping her in. Kyra gasped when she saw Sofia.

"Who's that?" Sofia asked.

"It's me, Kyra. I'm here to help." She reached out and, with a gesture of reassurance, gently touched Sofia's arm, though she recoiled.

From behind them, one of the men shouted, "Get a move on, Drake. Get yourself back here."

"Don't rush me. I've told you, I'm not going to run."

Caleb had difficulty putting on Sofia's seatbelt. He wasn't able to control his fingers; they were shaking too much. Eventually, Kyra had to help.

He knew he was playing for time, hoping there would be a chance, maybe a tiny opportunity where he could get away with them, too. But the area all around the car had no cover. Kev's men could see him the entire time, and there was nowhere for him to go. He had to resign himself to leaving her.

"I'm sorry, love. I've got to go. But, you know how much I

love you, don't you?" He leant into the car and kissed her. A long lingering kiss to say goodbye. For how long, he wasn't sure.

It took all of his determination to pull away from her as she screamed, "Don't leave me, Caleb. Please."

He closed the door, which Kyra locked as soon as Caleb had shut it. Despite her frailty, Sofia started banging and clawing on the window, wailing Caleb's name. Watching her, he almost lost his resolve and began looking around, searching for an opportunity to escape. It was futile. The gang would be on him before he'd even walked a few steps, and then they would go after the girls.

With every fibre of his body screaming with heartache, Caleb banged on the roof of the car and shouted, "Go!"

30

Moving as fast as she could, though driving safely, Kyra got away from the warehouse and onto a well-lit, busy street before stopping. She wanted to say something to comfort Sofia, who huddled in the passenger seat, quietly whimpering, in an obvious state of shock. But first, Kyra phoned the police.

She asked for Detective Reeves then hastily told him what had happened and where to go, reiterating it was an emergency, they needed firearms, and speed was of the essence. Only then did she turn to Sofia.

"I'm taking you to the hospital to get you checked out. The police are going to find Caleb, but my first job is to get you somewhere warm and safe." She reached out and gently touched Sofia's arm, as her words had elicited no response at all. This time Sofia didn't even flinch at Kyra's touch.

Arriving at the hospital, Kyra explained the situation to the nurses, telling them that Sofia had been abducted and that she didn't know what had happened to her during that time. A nurse helped Sofia into a wheelchair and took her away to assess her condition, telling Kyra they'd call her when they were ready.

Kyra took the opportunity to ring Nils to update him about what had happened.

"Shit, Kyra. What the hell were you thinking? Anything could have happened to you."

After his outburst, silence followed as Nils tried to control himself.

"I'm sorry. I can't imagine what I'd do if anything happened to you. Are you okay?"

"I'm fine. A little high on adrenaline, but physically, I'm okay. Sofia is in a bad way. They've taken her off to check her out. Can you ring Lukas and tell him what's happened, please?"

"Will do. Do you want me to come to the hospital?"

"No, I'll be fine on my own. There's nothing you can do, anyway. I'll ring you if there are any major changes. Otherwise, I'll see you later."

Around half an hour later, the nurse who'd already spoken to Kyra came back to see her.

"We've admitted Sofia for the night. Not surprisingly, she's exhausted, but apart from a few minor bruises and some superficial cuts around her wrists, she's fine physically, and so is the baby. You can see her, but she may be a little woozy. We've given her some medication to help her sleep and give her time to recover from the shock."

"She's pregnant?"

"Oh gosh, I assumed you knew," the nurse said, looking awkward. "When we mentioned it to her she didn't react, so we assumed she already knew – and you too. You're the best friend, right?" Kyra raised her eyebrows.

"The poor girl," the nurse said. " She must have been through a terrible ordeal."

"She certainly has." *Losing her husband and now possibly the real love of her life, too.* Kyra couldn't imagine the grief she must be suffering, and if she'd registered her pregnancy at all, how would that make her feel? "I'll just check in on her, if that's okay, and then I'll go home."

The nurse led her into the room where Sofia lay on her side, curled up in a ball.

Kyra sat beside the bed and gently reached out her hand to touch Sofia's. There was no response, so she whispered, "Get some sleep, and I'll see you tomorrow."

For the first time, she felt sympathy for Sofia, and then immediately guilty for not having considered her feelings during the last few weeks.

As Kyra left Sofia's room, she saw Liam Reeves coming through the entrance to the ward.

"Did you find them?" Kyra asked.

"No, I'm sorry. The place was empty and they'd done a good job of clearing away any forensic evidence, too. It's going to be hard to find where they've taken him. We're checking all the surrounding CCTV for any vehicles entering or leaving that site over the last week, and then see if we can trace their movement from there, but it could take some time."

"I'm not sure Caleb will have much time. This is revenge for Tony Johnson's imprisonment and death. Poor Sofia, she lost her husband and now she's lost Caleb."

"You look like you need a drink, though coffee is all I can offer in here. I'm going to interview Sofia, if you can wait?" Liam said.

"She won't be up to it. They've given her sedatives, because she's in shock. You won't get much of a response, if any."

"Okay, let's get that coffee and you can update me. Or would you prefer something stronger?"

"Thanks. Something stronger, I think – I need it."

"Whose car did you come in?" Liam asked.

"Caleb's."

"Give me the keys. I'll get Forensics to go over it. You never know, they might find something useful."

Kyra handed over the keys and Liam drove them to the nearest decent pub.

Liam ordered a large G&T for Kyra and a pint for himself. After he'd given her time to relax, Liam asked Kyra to give him a brief rundown of what had happened. Then he asked her if she, Nils and Lukas would go into the station the next day and give him statements about what had been going on since Caleb had appeared on the scene.

~

When she eventually arrived home in a police car that Liam had arranged, Nils rushed to the door to meet her. He pulled her into his arms and hugged her so tightly she could hardly breathe, partly due to his jumper smothering her.

"Nils," she eventually gasped.

"Sorry. My God, Kyra, I'm glad you didn't tell me what you were doing." He kissed her then held her away from him. "You stupid woman! What would I have done if anything happened to you? Didn't you think about me, how I'd feel?"

Kyra looked up at him. She'd never seen Nils like this before, in a seriously emotional state. Uncertain if he was truly angry, worried or both, she asked, "Why are you so emotional?"

"Because I'm relieved you're okay, and because – because I love you. You stupid woman."

This time he gave her a much longer and deeper kiss.

"I love you too, my Viking. We're so lucky to have found each other."

Nils picked her up in his arms and carried her to bed, leaving Kyra relieved he'd spared her any more questions.

31

Liam had asked Kyra, Nils and Lukas to meet him at the police station around eleven o'clock, but before that, Kyra wanted to go and visit Sofia to see how she was doing. Nils tagged along with her but, at Kyra's request, stayed outside Sofia's hospital room when they arrived.

"She's incredibly vulnerable at the moment. She's probably taken in the fact by now that she's pregnant. So, I think I'd better talk to her alone. Do you mind?"

"No. You're right. She doesn't want me lumbering in there. I'll sit and read, no worries."

Kyra kissed him and disappeared into Sofia's room.

Sofia, although awake, stared out of the window, and when Kyra spoke, Sofia showed no hint of recognition of someone else being in the room.

Kyra tried again, and sitting next to the hospital bed, reached out and tentatively held Sofia's hand.

"Hi, Sofia, how are you doing?"

Slowly, Sofia turned her head and focused on Kyra. Tears began to seep from her already red and swollen eyes. She whispered, "Thank you."

Unusually, Kyra was lost for words and it took her a while to speak.

"What have they told you about your condition?" Kyra asked.

Sofia looked even sadder, if that were possible.

"You mean about the baby?"

"Yes. Did you know?"

Sofia breathed in deeply, and again, silent tears fell.

"Not really. Things had been so weird, I hadn't really taken notice of what was happening to my body." She stopped talking. After trying to calm herself and failing miserably, she broke down completely.

Between sobs, she asked, "What am I going to do? They're both gone."

Kyra put her arms around Sofia, who, in turn, surrendered to her embrace, her whole body shaking as she cried.

Finally, she managed to slow her breathing and control her crying.

"I suppose you think I deserve this, don't you?"

"God, no, Sofia. Of course not. None of us know what you've been going through, but when you're strong enough, will you explain to us what happened between you, Cole and Caleb?"

With a look somewhere between resignation and gratefulness, Sofia nodded.

"I'm going to leave you to rest. Nils is outside and we're going to the police station to give our statements about what's been happening. I know Detective Reeves will want to speak to you too – when you're stronger. I'll check up on you later, okay?"

Again, Sofia nodded. "Thank you for saving me, Kyra."

When Kyra found Nils, he was engrossed in a magazine, but when he saw her, he stood up and took her in his arms.

"I can't even comprehend what she must be going through,"

Kyra said. "I know we've all had some negative thoughts about her over the last few months, but I feel so sorry for her." She held Nils tightly, grateful for his love.

Later, they met up with Lukas. Liam questioned them all about what had been happening over the last few months, since Cole's accident. After hearing their evidence, or more to the point their lack of it, he said he understood why they hadn't come to him before. There would have been no chance of him getting Forensics to do a DNA test on a bone without some serious evidence or funding. So he said it was a good thing they'd had the means to arrange private testing. He also hadn't known about the new genome tests. Like Caleb, he'd thought identical twins shared the same DNA.

Although they were still waiting for the DNA results, they were no longer required, as events had moved quicker than science and Caleb had exposed his own deception.

Liam, like Nils, reprimanded Kyra for agreeing to Caleb's plan to save Sofia rather than call the police. She pointed out that she'd got in contact as soon as she'd been able, but Liam still wasn't very impressed.

However, Kyra did have one useful piece of information for him. The name of Lenny's informant who worked as a LIO in the police, who obviously had contacts with the Johnson gang. She was the only one who had access to the files that Lenny had been interested in, and she'd told Lenny that she often spoke to some of Tony Johnson's crew.

"You might just have regained your credibility there, Kyra," Liam said.

After they'd all been interviewed, Lukas asked Nils and Kyra if they'd like to join him and Jess for lunch. He'd booked a table at James Martin's restaurant.

"What's the occasion?" Nils asked.

"Wait and see."

Kyra and Nils exchanged quizzical looks.

They arrived to find Jess already sitting at the table and sipping a glass of prosecco. After exchanging kisses and hugs, they all sat down.

Kyra let out a scream. "Oh my God, you haven't?" She grabbed Jess' left hand, admiring the sparkly, new diamond engagement ring adorning her fourth finger. Jess stretched her hand out for Nils to see too. He added his own congratulations, just as a bottle of champagne arrived at the table.

"When we got back from Ethiopia, I proposed," Lukas said. "I never want to be without Jess ever again. She's stood by me through these last months, when I must have been a right pain." He reached out and took Jess' hand. "Now I know what it feels like to be truly loved, warts and all. Looking back to the whole *Aliciana* affair, I should have been more mature. I should have supported Jess throughout that time, and I'm ashamed that I didn't—"

"You did when it mattered," Jess said, interrupting him. "And, besides, we weren't really together then. It was very early days in our relationship."

Kyra said, "You supported her when it mattered – that's the main thing. Congratulations to you both." Then, as an afterthought, she added, "Have you told your dad yet, Jess?"

"No, we're going to give him a call later. I know he'll be very happy. He loves Lukas."

"I know it may not be the right time to be celebrating, after what's happened to Sofia and Caleb, but, well, we thought that might be a good reason to celebrate. A time to be grateful for what we have and for the friends we have." Jess finished talking and held up her glass. "To good friends."

They all joined her in the toast.

Looking over at Jess, who gave him an encouraging nod, Lukas said, "Just one more thing. Nils, will you be my best man when we get married?"

Nils leapt to his feet and gave Lukas a bear hug that left him gasping for air.

"Of course, it'll be an honour. Erm, here in the UK or Sweden?"

Lukas looked over at Jess, and together they answered, "Sweden of course."

Nils cheered, then made another toast; they all clinked glasses before settling down to the important task of choosing their food.

32

A week later, having been released from the hospital and questioned by the police, Sofia had slowly started to come to terms with her ordeal. The hospital had arranged for her to see a counsellor each week, and the sessions seemed to be helping. However, there was no news about Caleb, and although she tried hard not to think the worst, she couldn't stop her mind from doing just that.

She rang Lukas and invited him, Jess, Nils and Kyra around so she could tell them the story about Cole and Caleb's background and their life in Liverpool.

When they'd all arrived, Sofia poured everyone some wine, though to Lukas' apparent surprise, she drank orange juice. "Because of the baby," she told him.

Once they were settled down, Sofia started her story.

She talked about the area they'd grown up in: a very tight-knit community of down-to-earth, working-class people. Most people didn't go to university when they left school, but Cole had been one of the few who had done.

She, Cole and Caleb had all attended Anfield Community Comprehensive School, although the twins were two years older than her. Everyone knew them at school, not just because they were identical twins, but also because they were so different from each other. Cole, the academic twin – keen on books, always worked hard, rarely in trouble; Caleb, also very bright, and sporty too – but he always got in trouble. He hated being likened to his twin, who had ambition. Caleb rebelled against everyone and everything.

"Obviously being identical, I thought they were both good-looking. I found their green eyes very attractive, but I fancied Caleb more because of his livelier character. Always funny, and liked to party, which Cole never did. At school, I used to get invited to a lot of parties, and that's where I met Caleb – at a party that one of my friends held."

Sofia smiled. "He was so hot. We got together during the night and afterwards he took me out again, and eventually we were seeing each other regularly."

She took a drink of her orange.

"My dad wasn't happy about me going out with a lad older than me. Mind you, he hadn't known about the others before Caleb! Anyway, my dad used to knock my mum around, so to escape the vile environment, I started going around to Caleb's. Often, his nan didn't even know we were both there. He'd sneak me in. But I felt safer at theirs than I did at mine. I'd often stay over, and either his nan didn't know, or turned a blind eye. I thought about him all the time and could never get enough of him—"

Jess interrupted. "So, you always fancied Caleb first?"

"Definitely."

"Why were they living with their nan?" Lukas asked.

"Because their mum, Belinda, was a drunk. After she had them, she just couldn't cope, and when they were little, they'd often be found left in the house on their own. One of the neighbours told the council, and they sent social workers around. They wanted to take the twins away from Belinda, but her mum, Betty, took them in and cared for them. She's great."

"And what happened to Belinda? Do you know why she committed suicide?" Kyra asked.

"I'll explain that in a minute. I need to tell the story in order."

Kyra nodded, and Sofia continued.

"About a year and a half after we'd started seeing each other, we began to drift apart, and I didn't see as much of him. I still saw him at school sometimes, but he often didn't bother turning up. I couldn't let go. I chased him, often texting him, but he seemed to have lost interest in me. Anyway, then I heard that he'd started going around with a gang, and it wasn't long after that he got arrested for the heist. You know all about that. That's when he went to prison. Though what you probably don't know is that Caleb didn't really know what the gang were into. He was horrified when he found out about the sex trafficking. I know he broke the law, but he didn't fully understand what he was getting involved in. That's why he gave evidence against them."

Sofia took another drink and took the opportunity to ask if anyone else wanted more wine.

After topping up Nils' and Lukas' glasses, she told them about Caleb's fake death and how he'd set that up, and why.

Nils asked his first question. "What happened to his friend Jaz?"

"I don't know. As far as Caleb knows, he managed to set up a new life and is still safe, but I don't know if that's true or not."

"He was brave helping Caleb. Going against his own family," Nils said.

"I know. Caleb thought of him like a brother. Anyway, you know what happened in Ethiopia, that Caleb changed places with Cole. When he came back, I didn't know for quite a time. I just thought that the accident had made him rethink things.

Though when I did know, I couldn't turn him in, because I've always loved Caleb, deep down."

"So, why did you marry Cole?" Lukas asked.

Sofia considered her answer before speaking. "When we heard about Caleb's death – that's when his mum committed suicide. As I said, she suffered from alcoholism, but then his death pushed her over the edge. Cole grieved for both her and Caleb, and I was devastated about Caleb's death. We started comforting each other. Well, Cole supported me more, but gradually over time, we became closer and closer. I moved in with him and then when he finished his course, as you know, he asked me to marry him." Again, she sipped her orange. "Selfishly, I wanted to get away from Liverpool and my family. Cole offered me a good quality of life." She paused. "Don't get me wrong, I did love Cole, and I was lucky, because I know he loved me. But, after the accident, when I recognised Caleb, it just reignited the fact he is my true love. That's why I couldn't give him away. I'm sorry." Sofia looked at Lukas when she said this.

She looked at them all to see their reaction. Only Lukas looked unconvinced, obviously still finding it hard to comprehend her actions.

"Now I'm praying that the police will find Caleb and get him back to me."

Kyra spoke first. "We hope so too, Sofia."

"Thank you for sharing the story. Now we can see it is more complicated than we could ever have imagined. I'm sorry you had to go through all of that," Jess said.

As they left, Lukas said to Sofia, "I am sorry that you were in the position you were, but I also hope you understand my reasons for being so upset. Cole was my best friend, and I still miss him every day. But, I hope that Caleb is found and you can welcome your baby together."

With tears in her eyes, Sofia said, “Thank you, Lukas, that means a lot to me.”

33
OCTOBER 2023

As each day passed, any hope of finding Caleb alive diminished, and Kyra was kept in the loop about each step of the investigation.

Immediately after his disappearance, the police had put out an APB to all seaports and airports in case the gang were trying to take him out of the country. Plus, officers had painstakingly searched through hours of CCTV to see if they could track the gang leaving the old docks, but with no success. The gang were far too organised and experienced.

A couple of days later, Caleb's body was found by a dog walker, who happened to be walking alongside part of the canal in a quiet area of the city, quite a way from the docks. And when the police turned up to the area while they were searching for evidence, they also found another body, later identified as Jaz Johnson.

Liam contacted Kyra to tell her and ask her if she would accompany him when he went to Sofia's, so that she wasn't alone when he gave her the news.

"They got their revenge, Kyra. They tortured him before killing him. He must have had a very painful death. I'm hoping that you won't mind me asking, but would you go with Sofia to identify his body? I think it's going to be extremely hard for her, and she doesn't seem to have anyone else."

Kyra said she would and agreed to meet Liam at Sofia's.

Sofia was inconsolable when she heard the news. In reality, she had known it unlikely that Caleb could have got away, but she'd had to retain hope. The fact that Jaz's body had also been found just added to her heartbreak. She knew his death would have broken Caleb, and she prayed that he hadn't witnessed Jaz's murder, although knowing what she did now of the gang, deep down she thought it most likely that he had. Both she and Caleb owed so much to Jaz, and although she'd never met him, she felt devastated that the gang had taken his life too.

Accompanied by Kyra, Sofia went to identify Caleb's body, and was heartbroken when she saw the damage to his face and relieved she didn't have to see more of his body. She could only imagine what other horrors they'd inflicted on him.

Kyra took Sofia home and encouraged her to take one of the sleeping pills the doctor had prescribed for her after she'd been abducted. Kyra then rang Nils to tell him she was staying over at Sofia's and she'd see him in the morning.

Later in the week, Liam got in touch with Kyra again, to tell her that, incredibly, the gang hadn't been quite as clever as they thought they'd been. When they'd taken Caleb, he'd put up a good fight, and under his nails, they'd found a tiny bit of skin, and the DNA led back to Kev, Tony's right-hand man. The gang must have completely forgotten about that when, later, they'd beaten much of Caleb's body to a pulp. They'd obviously assumed they'd destroyed any forensic evidence.

Then the police had yet another piece of unexpected good luck. The pathologist had been able to give an approximate time of death. This meant that when they captured Kev's car on CCTV in the vicinity of where the body had been discovered, they could prove he was in the area, and they were able to piece things together. By the time they'd finished, the police had enough evidence to arrest and question not only Kev but also several other members of the gang, who'd also been caught on various CCTV systems around the same area. Part of their downfall had been that, after killing Caleb, later in the evening, they'd all met up at a local pub to celebrate, and had even been overheard talking about what they'd done.

Like Caleb before him, Kev gave evidence to the police that meant the Dutch police could finally get warrants to arrest Marius de Haan and his whole team.

Caleb's death in a bizarre way had brought down a drugs-and-human-trafficking organised crime gang. Although Sofia was completely consumed with grief, Kyra hoped that she'd eventually recognise one little glimmer of light: Caleb's death had been the catalyst for the vile gang's demise.

Liam had also been in touch with Sofia to reduce her burden of stress. He told her that, although she'd broken the law by helping Caleb impersonate his brother, it was highly unlikely the CPS would charge her, because she had acted under duress.

Sofia confided in Kyra that, after the terrible news of the last few days, the only thing keeping her sane was the knowledge that she had part of Caleb growing inside her.

"I'll soon give birth to his child," she said, falling into Kyra's arms.

EPILOGUE: NOVEMBER 2023

Sofia invited Kyra, Nils, Lukas and Jess to join her to celebrate Cole and Caleb's lives. She had invited their nan, too, but she sadly didn't feel up to the journey. Happily, she and Sofia were now on good terms.

Sofia had visited Betty to tell her about Cole's accident and explain what had happened. She'd asked Kyra if she'd go with her, in case the news affected the twins' nan to the point of making her ill. Kyra had agreed and was impressed by the tactful way Sofia broke the news.

Despite her grief, Betty forgave Sofia for not getting in contact earlier, and having heard why Caleb faked his death, she understood and forgave him too. She regretted not visiting him in prison, but she'd been too angry with him, especially when Belinda had killed herself. But now, with the wisdom of age, she understood how they were all events completely out of her control. She was particularly grateful that Sofia had visited her personally to explain everything, and was overjoyed when Sofia told her that when the baby arrived, she'd bring the child to visit her.

With tears of happiness in her eyes, she said, "Thank you, Sofia. I feel that at last I'm going to get some of my family back."

Sofia hadn't been to church for years. She had been brought up in the Catholic faith, but hadn't been to a service since leaving Liverpool. Recently, she'd started going to Mass at a Catholic church not too far from the apartment. Father Donal, one of the young priests, hadn't been in the parish that long but had been very supportive of her memorial celebration for the twins. He wanted to build up the congregation with younger people and wasn't as judgemental as many older, more traditional priests might have been about her situation.

Sofia had Caleb cremated, with Betty's consent. Cole's body hadn't been fully recovered and remained somewhere in Africa, but his femur was buried with Caleb's ashes, in a spot marked by a memorial stone in a local cemetery near their apartment in Manchester.

Initially, Lukas wasn't keen to attend, even though he had more understanding of Sofia's actions after she'd shared the background of herself and the twins. However, when Kyra and Nils said they were going, Jess managed to persuade him that they should go too.

To his surprise, the whole event was very tastefully organised, and after a private, short memorial service at the church, the five of them had travelled to the cemetery where the memorial stone had been laid.

The wording on the stone also turned out to be totally different to what Lukas had imagined. The words were simple and beautifully elegant, and the stone itself, a beautiful piece of granite, with the words carved in gold.

In memory of

Cole Drake June 18th 1998 – April 10th 2023

Caleb Drake June 18th 1998 – October 12th 2023

Brothers, much loved in life and death.

Standing in the biting cold, each of them laid flowers by the memorial before going back to Sofia's for drinks.

Once in the apartment, Kyra and Jess helped Sofia set the food and drinks on the large island in the kitchen. Lukas and Nils stood admiring the view across Manchester. Nils hadn't been to the apartment before and was impressed.

"It's almost as good as yours," he said to Lukas. "Who bought their apartment first, you or Cole?"

Lukas looked thoughtful. "You know, I think, Cole. He and Sofia got married when we'd finished uni, when Jess and I were still living in Fallowfield."

They were interrupted by Sofia. "Come and get something to eat and drink. Hopefully it'll warm us all up." She encouraged everyone to dig in.

"So, what are you going to do now, Sofia?" Kyra asked.

"I'm hoping to stay here. I want to see how it goes with the baby. Maybe once they come along, I'll perhaps think about moving somewhere with a garden. I'll wait and see."

"When's baby due?" Nils asked.

"April, so I've quite a way to go yet."

"Are you worried about being on your own?" Jess asked.

"Not really. I've made a few friends at the antenatal meetings I go to, so I won't be completely alone. And Betty, the boys' nan, is going to keep in regular touch, although she won't be able to see me, unless I go to her. She's not doing so well these days when it comes to travelling. I've promised her, though, that when the baby's here, we'll go over and visit."

"I'm glad you were able to connect with her, and thank you for taking me with you," Kyra said.

Sofia gave her a hug. "No, thank you for supporting me – again."

Considering Lukas hadn't wanted to go, he was pleased that he'd gone. By the end of the afternoon, they were all laughing and getting on well, and any animosity in Lukas' heart had long dissipated. Sofia had changed, and she no longer seemed to be the selfish young girl she had appeared when 'Cole' had been flown home after the accident. Part of him couldn't quite believe it, but deep down, Lukas felt glad that the five of them could now all be friends.

"We'll all be here to support you if you need it, Sofia," Lukas added, looking at the others, who nodded in agreement.

AUGUST 2024

In April 2024, Sofia's baby had arrived and now she and Nils and Kyra were together again in Stockholm for the wedding of Lukas and Jess.

The venue, a hotel that owned all the land on one of the smaller islands in the archipelago, had been taken over for the wedding of Lukas and Jess Anderson, paid for by James.

Initially, Jess hadn't been very happy when James and Karin offered to pay for the venue. She felt it was all a little ostentatious, and, besides, the father of the bride should pay for the wedding. That was the tradition. But after a conversation with Danny, she graciously accepted the gift, especially after hearing that James had spoken to Danny about it, not wanting to step on his toes.

When Jess had seen the venue, months before, she had been so grateful that James had offered the gift. On the day of the wedding, the beautiful flowers, decorations, lighting – everything – was what any woman would dream of for their wedding day. Walking into the ceremony room with Danny, holding on to his arm, she glowed with happiness and love, thankful to be embraced by such a caring family and friends.

After the ceremony and wedding breakfast, Nils and Kyra sat side by side taking turns to hold baby Cleo, both completely besotted with her. Sofia had given birth to her healthy daughter on April 8th. The spitting image of both Cole and Caleb, she had their green eyes. Sofia had chosen the name Cleo because it comprised letters from both Cole and Caleb's names.

"I'm going to tell her about her dad and his brother as she grows, and when she's older, I'll explain the more complicated story about the twin brothers who I loved," she told them as they were both cooing over the baby. "They won't be forgotten, and definitely not with your book coming out too." She smiled at Nils and Kyra. She had asked them to write a book which they'd titled, *Pretending to be Cole*, telling the story of her and the twins.

"I'm grateful for you telling our story. Some people will be shocked, but many will understand it is a story of love and loss and how love wins out in the end."

The three of them clinked their champagne glasses together – that Sofia's was filled with lemonade due to the fact she still breastfed Cleo took nothing from the joy of the moment.

The wedding certainly was a joyous occasion, with many of Jess' and Lukas' friends joining them from all over the world. Danny and Anna were sitting alongside James and Karin deep in conversation.

As the evening went on, people gradually drifted away, leaving just the people who were staying at the hotel. Lukas and Jess weren't going on their honeymoon straight away – they wanted to spend a few days with both families together.

The day ended with little groups of people sitting around the hotel gardens that overlooked the lake, drinking, laughing, chatting and soaking up the atmosphere of what had been a beautiful day.

Jess and Lukas joined Kyra, Nils and Sofia, who were also relaxing. Sofia had just returned after putting Cleo down. She had a baby monitor on the table next to her. They were chatting about how beautiful the day had been when she surprised them all.

"It might not be the right time," Sofia said, "but I don't know when will. So – will you four be Cleo's godparents?"

Up until that point, everyone had chatted away a little louder than normally, due to the amount of alcohol they'd consumed. A sudden silence descended. Sofia looked at them and continued. "You are now among my most favourite people and I know that both Caleb and Cole would love the fact that you would be supporting us."

"Wow, I didn't expect that. It's a very special wedding present, being asked to be a godparent. Thank you, Sofia." Jess kissed her, followed by the others, who also agreed to take on the precious role.

"You never know, it might be you two next." Sofia smiled at the newly married couple.

"If Jess is as happy with motherhood as you, then I can't wait." Lukas leant over and kissed his wife.

The day had been perfect as far as he and Jess were concerned, and this had just made it even more special.

Lukas grabbed his glass and held it high.

"Let's make a toast. To absent friends, lovers and fathers – Cole and Caleb."

ACKNOWLEDGMENTS

With huge thanks to the following:

- Patricia Helen MacKay for her first read through of the book and her feedback.
- Beta readers: Carolyne Crawford, Amanda Dear and Hannah Edwards.
- Charlott Fagergard – for making Swedish connections for me.
- Sofia Jegerborn – for background information about Stockholm and the area, even at times going out of her way to check information for me.
- Sophia Best – information about police procedure.
- Neil McCallum, author, for his knowledge about Ethiopia.
- My husband, Conrad, for the initial idea for this story. Without his input this book wouldn't have been written.
- Gavin Kemp for his technological help – very much appreciated.
- Claire Cronshaw for her indomitable editing.

He is Not Worthy

ECHOES OF DRWONING

Echoes of Drowning

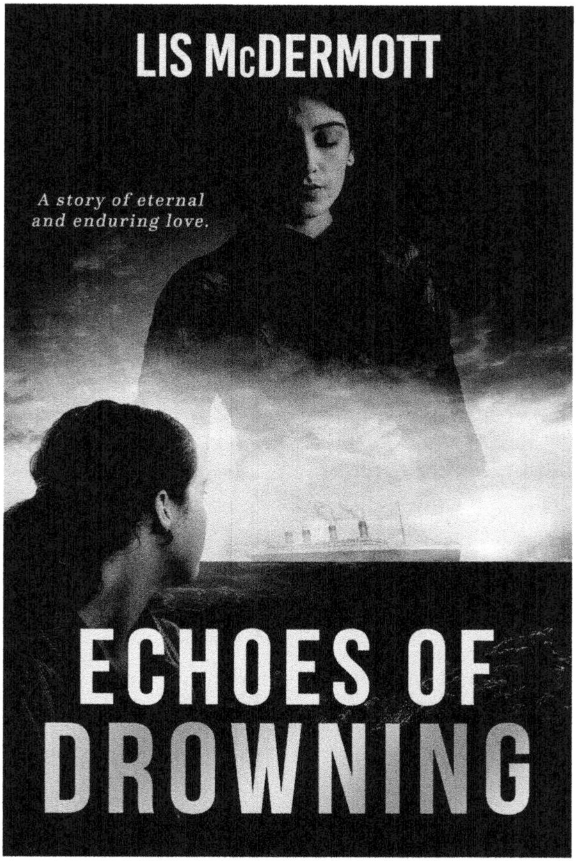

AUTHOR REQUEST

Hello,

Thank you for taking the time to read **Identity Enigma**.

- Rate or review this book on your favourite site.
- Tell your friends.
- Add it to a genre list on Goodreads.
- Connect with the author: friend, follow or like their fan page on Facebook.

Authors work hard to be noticed in the crowded world of books, and often it's word-of-mouth that makes all the difference.

Thank you for your support and help.

Lis McDermott

ABOUT THE AUTHOR

Lis McDermott spent thirty-four years working in music education, latterly as a schools adviser and OFSTED inspector, before leaving education in 2008 to set up her own photography business.

In the 90s, during her time in education, she co-wrote *Nelson Music*, a series of books to support the classroom music curriculum. She published her first solo book in 2014, a photography book called *Headshot Diva: why your business profile affects your bottom line.*

Having awoken another passion, she has now published an autobiography – a book of short stories and four poetry anthologies. She also mentors others to write their books.

Lis lives in Royal Wootton Bassett with her husband Conrad, with whom she shares a love of music and films.

facebook.com/LisMcDermottAuthor
x.com/LisMcDAuthor
instagram.com/lismcdermott
linkedin.com/in/lismcdermott

Printed in Great Britain
by Amazon

47267344R00128